Bruised, Resilient

MM Schreier

Published by Feral Phrases Press, 2024.

BRUISED, RESILIENT

First edition. September 27, 2024.

ISBN: 979-8991297806

Written by MM Schreier.

Table of Contents

For every woman who has laced her keys between her knuckles as she's walked to her car.

I see you.

Foreword

Years ago, I worked in a large industrial complex where my office was on the second floor. One afternoon, I complained to a guy friend, one who self-identified as a feminist and ally, that the elevator in my building always reeked of stinky feet. He laughed at me, asking if I was so lazy that I couldn't be bothered to climb a single flight of stairs. I explained to him there were no security cameras in the stairwells, so the elevator was safer.

He was floored. Not because he didn't believe me, but because he'd never really thought about the carefully curated vigilance that is a routine part of women's day-to-day activities. I didn't blame him. It was outside his lived experiences, and therefore out of mind.

It made me wonder why we don't talk about women's realities more openly. So, I decided I would.

What you'll find in the following pages are not necessarily stories *for* women, but *about* women. While sometimes told in a fantastical manner, the experiences are real. Be aware that some of this will be uncomfortable reading. I don't believe you can authentically explore women's experiences without talking about the horrific things men do to us, the unrealistic social expectations, the bullying, conditioning, and double standards. There's a lot of collective pain that women shoulder. However, there is strength and empowerment in these tales as well.

I hope that readers who identify as women will feel seen, and those who aren't women get a hint of what it's like to be one. Either way, may the words leave you thoughtful, a little angry, and a lot determined to help create a brighter tomorrow.

—MM Schreier, autumn, 2024

A Feast of Banalities

You can be anything you want.

Except an engineer—everyone knows girls aren't good at math. So she went into education, a socially acceptable field for the more compassionate, gentler sex. Taking a job as a kindergarten teacher, she buried her aspirations, feeding them to the tiny sharp-toothed monster that lived behind her breastbone. The creature devoured her dreams of designing robots while she wiped runny noses and sang the ABC song in an unenthusiastic, off-key monotone.

Behind every powerful man, there's a good woman.

Her mother told her it was better to be pretty than smart. How else would she catch a man? A dutiful daughter, she learned how to disguise her intellect and become a paper doll with a painted-on smile and a never-ending rotation of party dresses. The ravenous gremlin inside her chest gobbled up her witty repartee. Well fed on her curiosity, it grew from a fanged dust bunny to a wild-eyed ferret. All the while, she giggled and batted her eyes, obsessed over a white dress, and slipped on a gold ring so society would know her worth.

You don't know true love until you have a child.

She never really wanted kids but could never admit it out loud. Her loved ones would have been appalled. The world would have called her broken. Instead, she gave her terror to the inner ferret when she missed her period and convinced herself she'd change her mind when the baby came. Three months later, as the black blood gushed down her thighs, the critter feasted on her guilty relief and self-loathing until it swelled into a rabid badger.

Every storm cloud has a silver lining.

The one she was supposed to love most punched a fist-shaped hole in the drywall. She knew he didn't mean it, and when he apologized—and he always did, with flowers and a catch in his throat—she could still see the man she'd fallen for behind his eyes. If fleetingly. She weathered his insults and flash-bomb temper, for the monster was always there to consume the pain. Her beast-friend ate and grew, tentacles replacing bones, blood morphing to ichor. Still, it hungered.

Live, Laugh, Love.

Numb, she reached up to straighten the kitschy sign out of habit. Her sleeve fell back, showing a rainbow of fingerprints tattooed on her arm, blue, green, and fading yellow. The monster read the plaque's words through her eyes. It rumbled in discontent. Candy-scented emotions tasted sweet for a moment, but always soured on the tongue. She taught it that. It longed for something more substantial.

Asserting dominance, the creature raised her hand, knocking over a glass on the counter. Wine puddled on the marble like dark blood.

A spike of fear shot through her as she glanced over her shoulder, forgetting for a few heartbeats he was no longer there to blame her for the mess. The creature slurped up the anemic emotion. Too little. She had nothing more to give.

When the monster abandoned her, all that remained was a battered shell and the memories of who she could have been.

SafeChip(™)

Thea's SafeChip™ hadn't been working when it happened.

Three rapid blinks should have launched the ocular recording module. When her fear spiked, an automatic trouble ticket should have been filed with local law enforcement. As her heart raced and the pain tore through her, a first response team should have been dispatched to her GPS location.

None of that happened.

With the advent of SafeChip™ New York had become the safest city in the world. There was no reason why Thea shouldn't have taken the shortcut through the alley. She was in a rush to meet friends for lunch and had gone that way a hundred times before.

She had known her implant was faulty, but making an appointment to get it repaired was such a hassle. Refabrication and testing could take an entire cycle, and Thea was busy with her new teaching job. It wasn't that big of a deal—she didn't really need the Health and Security apps. She was young and hearty. Violent crime was nonexistent, a thing of long-forgotten folklore. It was law that all citizens maintained a functional chip and she had every intention of getting it repaired. It just hadn't seemed that urgent.

Until the incident.

Rough hands slammed her against the side of the building and her skull bounced off brick with a resounding thunk. Stunned, she struggled to focus. His leer swam in her vision, crowded with stained and crooked teeth. It was a hell of a thing to notice, but everyone had perfect smiles. Perfect skin. Perfect hair. Beauty was a programmed standard, enchanting features chosen à la carte from a menu of model-like ideals.

Shock masked the bite of the knife sinking into Thea's stomach. Things like that just didn't happen. It was unbelievable, and her brain was having trouble processing the sensation. Her body caught up when he pulled the blade out and the agony consumed her.

Blink. Blink. Blink.

Thea screamed when she realized no one was coming.

Her field of view narrowed to a pinpoint. His twisted sneer was the last thing she saw before the world went dark.

♀

A rhythmic beeping intruded on Thea's dreams.

She didn't want to wake. It was safe in the warm cocoon of blurred thought. A never-ending present buoyed her, sheltered her from her memories.

A bubble of sound enveloped her, floating toward the surface of reality. The swell shattered into fragments of whispered conversation. Disjointed phrases jabbed like icy shards pricking her consciousness.

...unknown stomach laceration... lost a lot of blood... SafeChip^{TM} *seems nonfunctional... lucky a passerby found... will have questions... highly unusual...*

Thea's eyes fluttered open. The hospital bed was tucked in a stark room, walls painted an immaculate, bleach-white. The monochrome purity irritated her; its brilliance felt like an illusion. An IV tethered her to the dinging, flashing machinery. She sucked in a deep breath and tasted antiseptic. Pain stabbed her side, and the bleeping became a jangled, insistent squalling.

"Try not to move."

The voice sounded bright but lacked depth. Its owner, a middle-aged man in an impeccable charcoal suit, sat stiff-backed in the plastic visitor's chair. His blonde hair was trimmed stylishly short.

"You've been through quite an ordeal." He grinned, thin lips pulled back from pearly, even teeth. It wasn't exactly friendly.

Thea's heart thumped, and the beeping mirrored her distress.

"My name is Agent Willis, from the Department of Anomalies." With a practiced flip of the wrist, he flashed a shiny badge. "Can you tell me what happened?" The man's eyes were jewel green and just as hard.

Thea swallowed. The words stuck in her throat. Would he believe her?

"I know this is difficult, Miss Martinez." He reached out and patted her arm.

Thea jerked away. Being touched by a stranger made her skin crawl. She wondered if she'd ever feel safe again.

The agent narrowed his eyes. "Tell me."

His stern command forced her to relive a chaotic jumble of images.

—Shade, the alley surprisingly cool after the blazing heat of the afternoon sun.

—Weathered and crumbling bricks scratching at her back.

—Breath that reeked of stim-fog smoke and something sour-sweet, like rotting fruit.

The small, specific details seemed so vivid. For some reason, the more important things escaped her. What had the man's face looked like, how tall, how old? What was he wearing? How long was the attack? Would she even recognize him if she saw him on the street?

"He laughed when he... s-stabbed me." The surreal word tangled on her tongue. "I'm sorry. It's all so unbelievable."

She couldn't remember if her purse had fallen from numb fingers, or if he had yanked it from her grasp. She choked back a sob.

"Why me? Why did I have to be the first...victim...in a hundred years?"

Her history degree served her well. Without it she wouldn't have had the words to define the experience.

Willis snorted, his lips twitching. Thea's jaw dropped as he rolled his eyes.

"Please." His voice mocked. "Everyone's a victim. You pathetic *sheep* just don't remember."

Thea wracked her brain, trying to make sense of the comment. Sheep—a domesticated ruminant animal with a thick wooly coat that had been raised for meat and fiber. Extinct. No, wrong context. Sheep—a person who is too easily influenced or led. Her stomach flipped, and a shudder ran through her.

"Ah. A glimmer of understanding. It's the SafeChip™ of course. Keeps the population compliant." His eyes were flat, as if talking of nothing more important than bugs. "Violent crime is worse than ever. Makes the 21st century look like utopia. Your implants rewrite your memories."

He got up and stretched his long legs. "It saves us millions on police investigations. And the nuisance of social justice warriors."

Heat burned Thea's face, and her jaw clenched. How dare they? She sat up, but something yanked her short. It took a moment for her to realize that she was handcuffed to the bedrail.

"Don't worry, sweetheart." Agent Willis fiddled with a knob on the IV. "Your implant will be repaired by the morning. You won't remember any of this...unpleasantness." He smirked and cranked the dial even higher.

Dizziness washed over Thea. She tried to fight it, but her eyelids drooped. A retort softened, melting away like mist in sunshine. Why was she mad again? Thoughts fuzzy and body languid, she slumped back onto the pillows. Willis's toothy smile followed her into her dreams.

♀

A rhythmic beeping intruded on Thea's dreams.

She fought against the sticky cobwebs of slumber. A scrap of a nightmare faded, banished to wherever forgotten memories went to die. The sensible part of her sighed in relief. She didn't want to remember.

Thea's head throbbed, and her side echoed it in a dull, persistent ache. An IV tethered her to the dinging machinery. Her thoughts felt muddled, and she reached up to rub her temples as if she could massage away a strange sense of déjà vu.

"Easy now. Try not to move too much."

A gentle hand touched her shoulder. She glanced up, and a tall man dressed in scrubs looked down at her. His brown eyes twinkled. Such a lovely, warm color. Maybe she'd get hers done. A little cosmetic bio-enhancement to celebrate her new job. Blue was so last year.

She shook her head, trying to order her wandering thoughts.

"What happened?" Thea remembered a sharp pain in her stomach, then the world had gone black.

"You collapsed on the sidewalk. The monitoring service sent out the call and the first response team arrived just in time. Emergency appendectomy." The nurse squeezed her hand. "Get some rest. You'll feel better in the morning. I say this all the time, but that implant saved your life today." He smiled again and left the room.

Thea snuggled into the fluffy pillows. Gratitude filled her. How lucky they all were to have the SafeChip™, to live in a world where everyone cared for each other. Technology was such an amazing thing. Her lips twitched up in a smile as she drifted off into a safe and dreamless sleep.

Things You Weren't Supposed to Hear (But Did)

Overheard in the locker room:
Have you seen the new girl?
The whale in glasses?

You draw your feet up so they don't know you're in the toilet stall. It takes a molasses-pulled eternity for their laughter to dissipate. You cut class. Phys ed sucks, and no one needs to see you in too-tight shorts, anyway.

Overheard at a frat party:
Dibs on the hot redhead.
Shit, that leaves me the chubby roommate.

You should've known but were flustered because he smiled at you. Countless retorts die on your tongue, leaving a sauerkraut tang behind. What's the point? You're nothing but a joke to him.

Overheard at the office:
Donuts in the breakroom!
Hurry, before the cow in accounting sniffs 'em out.

You rock back on your heels. You've never eaten anything but styrofoam-flavored rice cakes at work. It's important they know you're dieting. Thinness is a virtue. No matter how hard you try, it's never enough.

Overheard behind the curtain:

The patient is morbidly obese.
Needs to lay off the chips and get some exercise.

You just have a rash. Everything else looks good—blood pressure, cholesterol, sugars. What does that have to do with the strawberry bumps on your skin? Overweight isn't a diagnosis.

Overheard at home:

Silence.

You take a diet pill. Wash it down with low-calorie vodka. *Glutton. Pig.* Why not devour it all? You scarf down the pills, guzzle the booze—enough to make your heart stop hurting. Maybe after, they'll finally see you, not the fat.

The Lies I Tell Myself

There are a hundred and twenty-six squares on my bedroom ceiling. I've counted them. Twice. I tell myself I'll count them all again, as many times as I need to fall asleep. It's the kind of lie you tell yourself that rings hollow when you say it. Sort of like when you run into an old high school acquaintance at the grocery store, and you exclaim a little too enthusiastically that you *really must get together and catch up sometime.* Then you go home and stalk their social media—a beautiful family, a fancy house, vacations in the Caribbean—before deleting their number from your phone in a fit of self-loathing.

I stare at the ceiling.

One. Two. Fifteen...

Sighing, I acknowledge the lie, then throw back the sweaty sheets and slide out of bed. There's a crumpled pair of jeans in a heap on the floor, and I yank them on over my sleep shorts. I pause, but decide the oversized Ozzy world tour t-shirt left by an old 'friend with benefits' whose face I can barely recall is good enough. No bra. Mother would have been scandalized, but she's not here anymore to judge.

My sneakers are out by the front door. That means navigating the creaky stairs and the long hallway past Dad's bedroom. If he's taken his meds, he'll be so deep under a herd of water buffaloes stampeding through the dining room won't wake him. I can't risk that he hasn't spit the pills out, though. He says they give him weird dreams. Without the drugs, his breathing sucks, and even my careful footsteps could pull him from his fitful slumber. Then I'll have to tell him where I'm going in the middle of the night.

How does one explain they're off to view the *could-have-beens* to escape this miserable reality for a time?

I turn toward the open window. As I heave myself through, the rough wood scrapes across my belly. Great. Best case scenario, I'll be plucking out splinters. Worst case, a slow death from tetanus. Something to look forward to, then. I'm not suicidal. Just exhausted. And trapped in this monotony by decisions that I can't take back.

I push off the sill with my arms and land, the heat-burned grass prickling my bare feet. I've done it enough times that I've cleared all the jagged stones out from beneath the bedroom window. The bristly grass is the softest landing I'll get.

The street is quiet. Decent people sleep at this hour, or at least pretend to. I pass by the dark houses, slumped like fifty-something women with sassy haircuts and scarlet lipstick, trying too hard to disguise the fact they're past their prime. Bright curtains hang in spotless windows and the gardens are neatly planted with drought-tolerant flowers, but the siding is warped, and the catawampus roof shingles need replacing. I give the houses a smart salute. Solidarity ladies. I'm not quite middle-aged yet, but I feel like it.

Though it's been dark for hours, the day's heat still radiates from the sidewalks. At noon, the pavement would sear my feet, but here in the darkness, the warmth on my bare skin feels cozy. The breeze is still hot, though. It puffs against my neck like the fetid breath of some creepy monster, stalking me from behind. I don't look over my shoulder. If I don't acknowledge the beast, it can't be real.

Like a sleepwalker, I turn without thought. Left, right, left, left, through the intersection, beyond the park. My feet know the way. Muscle memory takes me past a shabby office with a faded sign reading 'Al's Budget Insurance.' I used to answer the phones there, one in a long string of minimum wage jobs, before Al had a heart attack and retired to Florida. Another casualty in a town where no one stays unless they have to.

I keep walking until my feet take me to the place I always end up, night after night.

The trains don't run anymore, and the station is boarded up to keep out teenagers looking for a place to party. Not that it stops them, drinking, that is. There are plenty of other quiet spots in this town, littered with empty beer cans and cigarette butts. I'm the only fool who keeps coming back to the deserted station.

I edge around the building and jump the turnstile onto the platform. A couple of green benches wait for passengers that no longer come. Oval patches of bare wood show through on the seats where countless backsides have worn the paint away. Some nights, I sit and do my part to increase the wear patterns.

Tonight, I pace as I wait.

Overhead, the full moon rises like a worn copper penny in a velvet sky. It doesn't fully illuminate the station, as if its pockmarked face is too tired to do its job. I don't need much light to see the derelict station. I know where the platform ends and the scrub grass grows up between the tracks, hearty weeds that seem indestructible, thriving in poor soil and almost no water, scorched by unforgiving heat.

The beast-breath wind rattles a yellowed paper notice pinned to the bulletin board. I can remember when the ancient station master would print out a new schedule and post it each Monday, even though the trains came at the same time every day. He was too set in his ways to figure out an electronic arrivals board. It wasn't long before the new highway made the trains obsolete, and the station had closed. Soon after, the old codger gave up the ghost, as if those weekly schedules had been the only thing keeping him going.

I stop pacing as the ground trembles beneath my feet. The tremble turns to a rumble. The uncanny earthquakes bring on the *could-have-beens*, an oasis in my desert. I wonder what the shockwaves will bring me tonight.

A second scene superimposes itself on reality. The station flickers between boarded-up and spit-polished windows, and a phantom sun shines in the night sky. Translucent figures bustle about, buying tickets and carrying luggage. Others sit on the empty benches. The clatter of wheels on the track and the shrill cry of the whistle echo quietly in the background.

I watch as a fifteen-year-old me slouches onto the platform.

"Stand up straight, Savannah." Mother's voice is stern but soft.

I straighten, hitching my backpack up on my shoulder, and she smiles. That slight quirk of her lips feels like diamonds or pixie dust, magical and rare. Perhaps when it's just the two of us, she'll be happier. Maybe if I improve my posture and have good manners, get good grades, and wear the right clothes, she'll be proud of me.

For a moment, I wonder what Dad will do without us. When I told him I wanted to live with Mother, he just looked me up and down and lit another cigarette. I knew what he was thinking—with Mother my nose ring, the dark eye makeup, the combat boots, they would all have to go. But at least he wouldn't keep me up at night anymore with his clinking beer bottles and wet, smoker's cough.

In the distance, the train barrels down the track, heading into the station. A flock of hummingbirds swoop and dive in my stomach, an odd mixture of fluttering wings and stabbing needle-sharp beaks. Mother reaches over to smooth a wrinkle from the gray skirt I'm wearing. The fabric itches and falls well past my knees, but she seems to like it. It's a small sacrifice, I suppose.

"When we get to New York, we'll get you fitted for your new school uniform." She smiles again and the hummingbirds melt away. "You're going to love it there. It's a great opportunity."

The earthquake stills and the *could-have-been* fades to tired reality. Ghost passengers disappear and the phantom sun gives way to the wan moon. Dust tickles my nose, and I stifle a sneeze. I flop down on one of the old benches and swallow down a lump in my throat.

She was right—the New York school was a great opportunity. Eighty-seven percent of the students got into Ivy League colleges, becoming doctors, lawyers, and important scientists. Everything Mother wanted for me.

Too bad I never went.

In the real world, when Dad asked me who I wanted to live with, I choked. He looked at me with those sad blue eyes, and I fucking choked. Mother was leaving him, and it seemed cruel for me to go as well. Besides, who needed all her stuffy rules? I liked my nose ring and my wardrobe of chunky boots and black jeans. Who cared about that fancy school up North?

So, I stayed. Barely graduated from high school and got a job bagging groceries. Drove Dad to his appointments when his license got pulled after too many DUIs. Got a second job waiting tables to pay the bills. Lost my virginity in the back seat of a rust bucket Chevy.

The ground rumbles again, and I bite back a curse. This time I know what's coming.

Jackson hands me my ticket. I grab the slip of paper, but he doesn't let go of his end right away.

"Will you put it on now, Savvy?"

I nod and pull out the ring I've been carrying around in my pocket. The band is thin, and the diamond is a tiny ice chip. It barely sparkles in the moonlight, yet somehow it feels heavy on my finger. The weight isn't just a symbol of commitment, but of a choice. The kind that changes lives.

A loud voice makes me jump. "All aboard for the midnight express to Memphis."

By the time the sun rises, we'll be in the big city. By the time Dad gets up and shuffles to the kitchen to find my note, Jackson and I will be married, ready to start a new life together.

I bend to pick up my bag, and the handle slips in my sweaty hand. It's hard to believe everything fits in a couple of secondhand suitcases. But how can you start fresh if you're dragging around a million reminders of your past?

Jackson slips a wiry arm around my waist and kisses the top of my head. I glance up. He has a strong chin and a hatchet nose that's too big for his face. But he's kind and full of big ideas. The sorts of ideas that would stagnate in a small town; ideas that need room to breathe and grow.

The whistle blares as Jackson takes my hand, helping me up the train steps. I don't look back. There's only forward.

Once again, the *could-have-been* fades. The train disappears; the weight of the ring on my finger evaporates. I rub my chest as if I can scrub away the hollowness that lives there. My bare toes hang over the edge of the platform, the weathered boards rough as a cat's tongue against my skin. I will the ground to rumble, but the quakes are done for the night, leaving me no wishful fantasies to lose myself in.

In reality, Jackson asked me to marry him the day Dad got his diagnosis. I had to choose between love and duty. Duty won. Jackson had his ideas and the world. He didn't need me.

Dad did.

It's not your job to take care of him, Jackson said. But if I didn't, who would?

The beast-wind pulls on my ponytail and whispers in my ear. I imagine it wonders why I torture myself, living out the *could-have-beens* instead of sleeping. I tell it the visions keep me sane, give me a moment of peace. A hope that alternate versions of myself chose better.

I shout into the wind that it's not about trying to see where Mother and Jackson might be now. That I won't use the clues from the visions to scour the internet and haunt their socials, like some pathetic stalker. Is she remarried? Does he have kids?

Do they ever think of me?

A smudge of rose light creeps over the horizon as I make my way home. I clamber through the open window and shuck off my jeans. The backs of my knees are damp with sweat and my eyes feel gritty after another night with no sleep.

I creep down to the kitchen and start the coffee, making it extra strong. I organize Dad's morning meds and pour a glass of water—room temperature, cold makes him cough and wheeze. A phlegmy hacking comes from the hall. It sounds worse than it did before.

Everything will be okay. I chant it over and over like a mantra until the words run together and lose meaning. The syllables circle in my head as I flip open my laptop and pull up Facebook. I'll just check my own feed.

More lies I tell myself.

A Taste of Online Dating

Gods, how I hate pantyhose. They itch and run. Resigned, I ease them up, careful not to snag the sheer fabric with my manicured nails. I cast a critical look at the full-length mirror. It is important to get the details right.

Lipstick next. I rummage through the tubes, countless shades of bronze and pink. No, red. Not a brazen crimson, but a deep, smoky cranberry. I slip into heels that pinch my feet—not too high, not too low. There's a fine line between sexy and slutty. Who makes these rules?

I smooth my dress over my thighs. It clings to my curves and accentuates breasts pushed upward, encased in a prison of lace.

Men's desires are tiresome.

I consider canceling, but my stomach growls. Hunger wins.

When I pull into the lot at the seaside restaurant, I suspect he's nearby, watching, and so I make a production of getting out of the car. Legs first, stretched to full length. Standing, I twirl my wrap, and with a graceful spin end up leaning against the car. I run fingers through my hair, angled into the sun so chestnut, wind-tousled curls gleam. It's a circus act and I am a master performer.

I sense a flare of emotion down on the beach—a complex recipe spiced with desire and nerves. I breathe it in. Damn, I'm hungry. Patience. It won't be long before he comes to me.

Movement draws my attention. I can feel his eyes on me, so I raise a hand in greeting. His long legs eat up the distance between us. As he rubs his palms on his pants, I can smell his anxiety. And his arousal.

"Emily? The photos don't do you justice."

I muster a girlish titter. He doesn't shake my hand, but simply cradles it as if it's a fragile baby bird. His pulse flutters as I trace my thumb along the inside of his wrist. I inhale his growing desire, and an ache blooms in my stomach. Knees tremble and I swallow hard.

Instead of going inside the restaurant, he suggests a stroll by the shore. I smother irritation—the sand will ruin my heels—and paste on a faux smile. Tucking my hand in the crook of his arm, I lead him around a rocky peninsula onto a stretch of deserted shoreline.

It lends some privacy for what's to come.

Milking a full-lipped pout, I pause by a tidepool and lean close to take a selfie, the two of us cheek-to-cheek. I like to keep trophies. The image on my phone reveals my true self. His eyes widen at the sight of my round, lipless mouth and rings of barbed teeth. Fear oozes from his pores, a delicious whiff tantalizing my palate. Unable to keep the hunger at bay any longer, I latch lamprey-like onto his temple to suck down the savory emotion.

I rummage through his memories, slurping choice morsels.

The church smells of lilies at his father's funeral.

His coworkers slap him on the back, congratulations for a job well done.

Walking across the stage to accept his diploma, the world is at his disposal.

The first blush of attraction turns heated, sultry.

A betrayal and a broken heart bring on years of darkness.

I gobble down the buffet of emotions, nibbling on his pain, pride, lust, joy. I cannot resist a second helping and delve deeper into his past.

Clutching a Superman lunchbox, he attends his first day of school. Another boy smiles, and he hopes they will be friends. In the afternoons, he romps with a fluffy puppy, watches cartoons, waits for Mommy to come home.

Soon, he's nothing but a void wrapped in flesh.

With a whisper in his ear, I fill the emptiness with a command. Zombielike, he shambles back to his car. Within moments, the engine rumbles and he's speeding up the switchbacks. Metal screams as he hurtles through the guardrail, flies off the cliff.

I turn away as the car hits the water, satisfied the remnants of my meal are tidied away. The rules say the female cleans up after dinner. More inane decrees. But one must follow society's expectations in order to fit in.

My pantyhose squeeze too tight; I've gorged myself. In the parking lot, I rip off the offending nylons and sigh in satisfaction. This world with its online conveniences pleases me. Why hunt when I can swipe right and a smorgasbord of lonely souls offer themselves to me? If I lick the screen, I can almost taste the desperation.

Sated, I put the convertible's top down and turn the key in the ignition. I want to feel the wind in my feathers. Hair. Whatever they call it.

The Surgeon and the Albatross

The wail of an ambulance tore through the night. Serena wondered why they always sounded louder when the air was frozen. She shook her head and exhaled. Foggy breath mingled with mentholated smoke, and she shivered in her thin scrubs, annoyed she hadn't taken the time to grab her gloves and jacket. She took another deep drag from her cigarette. These guilty pleasure minutes were worth the bad breath and chilled fingertips. Anything to get through another shift without cracking.

The siren screamed closer, accompanied by a blaring horn.

"Damn, they're coming in hot."

She sighed, knowing what came next.

On cue, her pager beeped. Serena didn't glance down as she thumbed the mute button. She ground the butt out beneath her heel and left the paper corpse alongside dozens of its fellows. Not all were hers, but few had been smoked to the filter. The pagers were demanding.

A quiver tickled Serena's stomach, a tangled mixture of butterfly wings and writhing serpents. Her moment of peace melted away as she turned to wade back into the familiar chaos inside the ER.

♀

The doppler is all-encompassing. It reminds me of a carnival—the curious marriage of squalling kids and too-jaunty carousel music. Voices and sensations ride below the clamor, but it's the siren that commands my reality. Pulled by the sound, we race toward a destination I hope to never reach. Where is immaterial. I'm just afraid that when we get there, the cacophony will abandon me and those things lurking underneath will rise to the surface. I don't want to feel them.

♀

The hot water thawed Serena's fingers as she scrubbed in at the deep stainless-steel sink. She glanced at the intern at her side and smothered a sigh. Juan was good at his job, but he always watched her with a shrewd look in his eye. As if waiting for her to screw up.

"What have we got?" Serena kept scrubbing as she waited for him to bring her up to date.

"Car accident. Guy's a mess. Drove into a bridge abutment going fifty. Girlfriend thinks he took something but doesn't know what. He coded twice on the way over. Paramedics intubated en route."

Serena opened her mouth, but Juan bowled over her.

"They did a good job."

She wanted to say—they better have—but bit the words back, afraid it would look snarky.

A crash of metal on tile drew her attention from the conversation. Surgical instruments littered the floor, and a sterilization tech froze under her glower, half-crouched to pick them up. His cheeks flushed scarlet.

Serena turned back to the sink and spoke into the stream of water as she rinsed.

"Get another set in here. Fast."

Juan didn't comment, but a muscle twitched in Serena's cheek as she held up her hands in front of her, elbows bent at ninety degrees. She hated that her clipped tone would invariably land on the staff's list of grievances. 'Doctor S snaps at technicians. What a bitch.'

Funny. The male surgeons never dealt with that kind of crap.

Serena squashed a flare of indignation at the double-standard and hip-checked the door to the operating suite—there was no room for emotions in surgery. She had a job to do.

♀

Breathing hurts. The rhythm's not my own. I want to stop, but the tube won't let me, forcing lungs to inflate like a balloon at a child's birthday party. No one asks the balloon what it wants. No one asks me. Someone thumbs my eyelids back, shining a light and stealing my darkness. If I could speak, I'd beg them to give it back. I crave the safety of infinite, inky oblivion. No blinding light, no piercing sounds, only the exquisite refuge of monochrome eternity.

Too many voices hum around me. There's singing, but I can't understand the words. Above it all, a serious stranger barks commands, as if she can change fate if she issues her orders with firm and sterile confidence. I'm not certain that she can.

♀

The sweet trill of a soprano drifted through the operating theater. Serena always played Puccini during surgery. Once she'd overheard an intern calling her pretentious, but the libretto of *La Bohème* or *Turandot* reminded her of her Nonna. When the music sounded, the phantom scent of oregano masked the burn of industrial disinfectants and calmed the surgeon's nerves.

For a tiny Italian housewife, Nonna had been a tempest: generous with her ladle, her hugs, and unsolicited advice. Serena could still hear the wizened old lady's voice in her head.

"Of course, you'll be a great doctor, bambina! Now have another meatball. You're too skinny." When she said it so matter of fact, it had sounded irrefutable.

Serena wished she had some of that confidence now; her rock-solid hands belied churning insides. Juan hadn't exaggerated when he'd said their patient was a mess. With the steering column jammed into the man's chest, the blinker lever had stabbed him like a prison yard shiv. Blood gushed and Serena couldn't see if it had pierced his heart.

"More suction."

It came out harsher than she'd intended. She cringed under her mask, hating that she needed to even think about that right now.

As the blood cleared, she took a closer look.

"Not good."

More like a fucking mess, she added in her head.

The back of her neck twinged as she hunched over the patient and concentrated. No one could fix this.

She had to try.

♀

Somewhere in the distance, a familiar voice howls. I should comfort her, tell her everything will be ok. Best to pat her on the arm, explaining it will all be over soon. She needn't waste her tears. It's better this way, even if she doesn't see it now. Her grief will fade and leave her unfettered, no track-marked albatross weighing her down.

I attempt to go to her, but my body is not mine to order any more. It hasn't really been mine for years, as if living has become muscle memory.

Still, at this moment, the habit no longer holds sway. The machines and the somber strangers are in charge now.

♀

Out in the hallway, hysterical wailing competed with Puccini's aria. The howls shattered Serena's concentration and set her teeth on edge.

"Somebody shut that woman up."

The crier's grief lodged itself in Serena's core, burrowing into her like an eel. It feasted on her confidence.

"Why isn't she down in the waiting room?"

Juan frowned. They both knew the answer. Sometimes in the chaotic rush to get a trauma patient to surgery, their loved ones trailed after the paramedics and got lost in the shuffle. He nodded at someone beyond Serena's line of vision, a silent directive.

The soprano belted out an impossible arpeggio and by the time she hovered on the top note the crying receded. Still, the doubt-creature remained entrenched in Serena's chest. It watched as she worked, silent and judging.

The heart monitor stuttered, and her mouth went dry.

"Damn it. We're losing him."

♀

*An insistent, syncopated beeping falters. Someone shouts—*clear!*—and lightning jolts through me. The faint scent of burnt hair lingers in my nostrils, but I don't feel anything. I'm divorced from my body.*

*The voices are muffled as if heard underwater. I step outside myself, and the beeping transmutes to a long, unbroken tone. From the other side, a sonorous hymn replaces the opera. It sings in my ear—*stretch your wings and fly, albatross. *I shrink away. I don't want to swoop and soar. Let me fall, for the choice I made is unforgivable.*

The doctors shock me again, and for a contrived heartbeat, my broken corpse tugs me back. Unrelenting machinery and faceless strangers battle to make me stay, but I will not be forced. My will wrenches free of their machinations, allowing me to sink into the bittersweet embrace of the void. I welcome the harmonious dark.

♀

The heart monitor flatlined in an unrelieved bleating.

"Time of death: zero three twenty-seven."

Puccini's cadenza faded into silence as Serena stripped off her gloves and stalked out of the room. She shouldered past the somber nurses and interns, her face stony. In the hallway, fluorescent lights pricked at her eyes to leave a blur of color in her peripheral vision. The paper mask fluttered against her mouth, and she tore it away, unable to breathe. Someone called her name, but she pretended not to hear.

Deep inside her ribcage, the doubt-creature gnawed with its sharp teeth. She wondered when the whispers would start. Not good enough to play with the Big Boys. Women don't have the chops to be surgeons. It didn't matter if she was the best. There was a dead guy on her table.

The door slammed behind her as she burst into the shadowed alley. Cigarette butt corpses glared at her from the pavement in silent accusation. An icy wind whipped between the buildings and scattered them in its wake.

Overhead, a halfhearted security light flickered and died. Wrapping her arms around herself, Serena stared up into an infinite black sky. She welcomed the darkness, grateful that no one could see the tears freezing on her cheeks.

Wine, Menopause, and Summoning Demons

The thing about hot flashes is no one mentions once your hormones yeet you from the center of the sun, you take an unexpected detour to virtual Antarctica where you freeze your tits off even though the 60-degree wine aging room felt like heaven five minutes ago. Luckily, the rows of oak kegs aren't too judgy of not-quite-fifty-I-swear ladies with indecently hard nipples.

I insert the wine thief in a barrel and extract a sample of the Cabernet.

Sniff, swirl, sip, swish.

I wrinkle my nose and spit. The wine is oaky, with a hint of horse manure. Don't ask me how I know what *that* tastes like.

Dammit.

Moving on, I try the Malbec.

Sniff, swirl, sip, swish, spit.

Donkey piss. For the record, I'm imagining that one.

It's bad enough I'm freezing my ass off, but discovering all of this season's wines are trash is worse. Between drought and wildfires, the grapes have revolted. It's going to ruin me.

There's still the Merlot.

I repeat the sniff, swirl, sip ritual, but before the liquid hits my tongue, the winery's mouser, Clawdia, weaves through my legs. Stumbling, I spray wine like a burgundy fountain and execute a complicated Cha-cha-cha trying to keep my balance. I suck in a ragged breath and swallow a bit of cat hair.

Very sexy.

Clawdia hisses and puffs up into an angry orange hairball. Her tail twitches as she glares at something over my shoulder. I turn.

A dumpy man wearing a pair of devil's horns tries to extricate a plastic pitchfork tangled in his blood-red satin cape. Where the hell did this dude come from and how much of that Cha-cha-stumble did he just see? And doesn't he know Halloween's not for another two weeks?

I muster my best customer service voice. "Hello. This area is employee-only. The tasting room is upstairs."

The man huffs and throws his cape inelegantly over his shoulder, before fixing odd yellow eyes on me. "I was minding my own business, sorting out Hell's requisition forms when *you* summoned *me*."

"Excuse me?"

This is a dream. I forgot to spit and am zonked out in a wine-scented stupor, never mind I have the tolerance of a middle-aged divorcee who owns a flipping winery, and did he just say summoned, what is going on—

The man reaches out and pinches my arm.

"Hey!"

He looks annoyed. "You were getting hysterical."

I snap out of it. "That's an offensive word." Mediocre white men and their misogynist labels. "Who are you, and what's with the cape?"

"Oh, sorry. It's 'Dress Like Dad Day.' The succubus in HR thought it would be a good team-building exercise."

He claps his hands. Suddenly he's in khakis and a tucked-in polo. Where the horns had been, an optimistic comb-over does little to hide a balding pate. He looks like an accountant. With goat-slitted eyes.

The odd little demon clucks his tongue. "Now, about the summons? I don't have all day, and those requisition forms won't sort themselves."

Demon. That's right, I went there. The thought should be terrifying, but he's no more intimidating than my dentist, and between menopausal crankiness and the wine crisis, I have no patience for sass.

"There's been a mistake. I wouldn't know how to summon a demon, even if I wanted to. Which I don't."

He cocks an eyebrow. "Three sips of wine, not meant to be consumed and some Latin American dance steps—"

"Cha-cha?" Dizziness turns me into a weeble-wobble, and I slump against the Merlot barrel. Damned hormones.

The demon taps his toes. He's wearing white Velcro support sneakers, so help me...well, invoking God feels awkward right about now.

"Cha-cha is fine. I prefer Salsa, but really anything will do. Top the whole thing off with the binding element—three cat hairs, swallowed whole." He brushes at his khakis. "Yours appears to be ginger."

Well, hell's bells. I've accidentally summoned a demon. I look around for Clawdia, but she's disappeared under the barrel racks. Traitor.

"Sure, all that happened, but it wasn't on purpose. Feel free to return to your forms. No need to stick around on my account." I'm too polite to say what I'm really thinking, *skedaddle, scram, vamoose!*

"Sorry, ma'am. Section Three-thousand-forty-eight B says a bargain must be struck before I can return to Hell. It's in the manual."

I sigh. Of course, Hell has a manual, and he doesn't seem much of a rule-breaker. Not even a little rule-bending. I shouldn't judge—I don't do a lot of bending (or squatting or twisting) these days myself.

"Fine. So, how does this work?"

"You make me an offering, I do something for you, and then I'm out of your hair." He flashes a tired smile. "I won't even try to trick you like a Crossroads demon. I'm just a purchasing clerk and want to get back to the office."

I scan the room. What does one offer an unexpected demon? There's nothing but the Merlot. I use the wine thief to decant a double pull—best be generous—then hand him a glass. The demon sips.

Sweat trickles between my boobs. I ignore the growing hot flash as I wait for the verdict.

He *swallows* instead of spits. Heathen.

"Delightful!" The demon grins. "Offering accepted. Now, what can I do for you?"

A million thoughts caper in my head. One doesn't often get a free pass, and I should make this good. Money? Fame? Inappropriately young men?

Heat bears down with the ferocity of the Sahara at noon. I need an oasis.

"How about banishing these menopause symptoms? You know, the hot flashes, brain fog, random dizziness, never-ending insomnia, bloating—"

He clears his throat. "Um, understood, no need for details."

I roll my eyes. Men can be so squeamish. The demon snaps his fingers, and I immediately feel clear-minded and blessedly cool.

"Bargain complete." Without another word, he disappears.

Well, that was abrupt.

For a few moments, I revel in my good luck. No more menopause, soul intact, and at least one vintage is salvageable. Accidentally summoning a demon is the best thing I've done all week.

I insert the wine thief, eager to taste the demon-approved, *delightful* Merlot.

Sniff, swirl, sip, swish, spit.

Yuck. It reeks of sulfur.

Dammit. I'm going to have to learn to Salsa.

To Catch the Wind

Ash's trembling fingers closed the laptop with a snap. How could such a thin metal square hold so much hatred? There was no way they could go back to school tomorrow. After sliding the computer into their backpack, they slowly tugged the zipper.

Snick, snick, snick.

As each tooth snapped into place, a phantom noose tightened around Ash's neck. Their heart raced and black flecks filled their vision.

What was that thing they were supposed to do? 'Name three things: something you can see, something you can hear, and something you can feel.'

Gasping, Ash glanced toward the open window.

See: curtains fluttering on an unexpected breeze.

Hear: their name whispered on the wind.

Feel: a cool draft on a feverish cheek.

♀

Green-thumbed gurus say gardening is therapeutic. I say it is war. Battles against weeds, skirmishes with rabbits. Strategies to counter a lack of rain and my aging body, rain barrels and kneepads. Constant digging in the dirt splits my fingernails and irritates the crepe paper skin on the backs of my hands. The books say I must connect with the earth, allow my energy to mingle with the soil.

It sounds hokey, but I'll try anything. I've already tried so much. This time, for sure. A mother never loses hope.

Patience has never been my strength, but the years have tempered me. I wait for the sunlight to morph from golden to indigo. It's said this must be done in that fleeting moment between sunset and twilight.

The herb knife weighs heavy in my hand, its short, curved blade razor-sharp. I peruse the garden trying to remember which plant is the one I need.

"Foxglove for vision." I reach for the spike of pink bells, then pause, gooseflesh prickling my neck. I'm forgetting something.

Foxglove enhances Sight by bringing visions of the underworld.

"Dammit! That's not it."

It's critical I get this right. There's not a lot of time, and if I miss my chance, I'll have to wait another year. My stomach churns.

A litany of flowers and herbs for Sight march through my mind. Kava kava for astral projection. Cat's Claw for shamanic journeys. Primrose for uncovering hidden truths.

Primrose.

I refuse to feel silly when thanking the plant for its gift as I fill my basket with butter-yellow flowers.

♀

The wind giggled and became a diaphanous girl dressed in cottony clouds, hair wild. Her edges roiled in a persistent blurring and reforming, while lightning flickered in her eyes.

Panic forgotten, Ash's jaw dropped.

Downstairs, adult voices rumbled. Ash couldn't take another dinner set for four—themself, Mom, Dad, and the ever-present anger.

The girl held out a hand. When she spoke, her voice sounded like the rustle of leaves.

"Come fly with me!"

♀

I drop the basket of flowers on the kitchen counter next to my phone without checking for messages.

At first, David would call every year on this day. Over time, his voicemails shifted from friendly check-ins to admonishments to move on. The final one lasted ten minutes, mostly in silence, while his new wife muttered about dinner reservations in the background.

I'm glad to no longer suffer the calls, but I cannot accept and forget like he has. A mother never does.

While the water boils, I wander the house. It's more a museum than home. It's not just nostalgia. My research says it's important to keep things familiar to make the transition back easier.

I touch each relic as I walk by. David's recliner, the leather worn and cracked. A pair of soccer cleats, size six, lined up in the front hall. A closed door to a bedroom I refuse to clean out. I press my forehead against the smooth wood and pray to gods I don't fully believe in.

"Please...just, please." I don't know how to say the words aloud.

The teakettle shrieks, echoing the silent screaming of my heart.

I hurry back to the kitchen to sort the primroses, placing thirteen perfect blossoms into a glass bowl. There's time for them to steep. Just barely.

♀

They swooped over treetops turned burgundy and copper. A promised kiss of frost followed in their wake, but the cold didn't touch them. They played a game with the old oaks, twining around branches, prying free bunches of leaves the dryads clutched in their twiggy fingertips.

Time passed in seasons. On a sun-warmed beach, they trailed feathery caresses across the shoulders of summer lovers. They howled merrily and danced to thunder drums. They painted windows with hoarfrost and chased fireflies through flowered bowers.

Strange words occasionally tickled their mind—home, mother, ash—but were easily dismissed as meaningless thought fragments.

♀

Outside, a round moon rises, casting a quicksilver stream through the glass sliders. I take it as an auspicious omen. Arthritis makes my fingers stiff as I knot a blue-patterned scarf around my throat for remembrance. An old birthday gift I hope makes up for the gray hair and extra weight around the middle. After all this time, I look different, but I'm still *Mother* inside.

I take the cooling primrose concoction, smear it over my eyes, and chant the incantation I've been practicing.

"Hic Tamen Non Hic Ostendo."

I repeat it until the words run together and my tongue dries. Shadows lurk in my peripheral vision, but I pay them no heed. I won't waste the Sight on boggarts and house spirits.

The silver net took me months of pain to crochet, sharp fibers bloodying my fingertips. Sacrifice is required to catch the wind. I gather the gossamer web to my chest and shuffle out into the moonlight-drenched yard. It is time.

The sylph is already there, circling the garden. It ruffles the zinnias, making their colorful heads bob to some unheard song.

I ready the net. I'll needs be quick.

The wind creature swirls around me, and I blink back tears as I see in its heart a familiar, if translucent, face. Sharp cheekbones, just like their father's. Deep-set eyes, just like mine. The dark circles are gone, though.

Ash smiles.

I don't remember them so radiant. My heart squeezes in my chest; the net slips from numb fingers. It's taken me twenty years to understand.

In flight, they are free.

I watch until the primrose magic fades, and there's nothing left to see but the dancing flowers.

For Want of a Conversation

Granny Kerson puttered around her kitchen making breakfast. One poached egg on a slice of multigrain toast. Same thing she had every Sunday. The rest of the week, she made do with a bowl of plain oatmeal. She used to have bacon and grapefruit and flaky, buttery chocolate-filled croissants, but food just didn't taste the same since Alfred passed away. Besides, it was no fun making fancy meals for one, or sitting in silence, eating alone. Her husband had been an excellent conversationalist.

She huffed as someone outside honked. Twitching the kitchen curtain aside, she saw the new neighbors—she could never remember their names—bundling their children into their car. Granny frowned. Where were they off to at this hour? They weren't really the church going sort of family.

Neighbor-wife kept stealing anxious glances at the sky as Neighbor-husband shoved a couple of suitcases in the trunk. Ah, vacation then. Granny hoped for their sake they weren't headed to the beach. It was dimmer out than usual for this hour, probably a storm coming. She didn't search the sky for thunderheads, though; looking up triggered her vertigo. No sense wasting the day stretched out on the couch to check for a storm she didn't really care about. With her arthritic knees, it wasn't like she had a hike up Kilimanjaro planned. Even a short jaunt around the block aggravated the aches and pains.

The tea kettle whistled, and Granny smoothed the drapes back in place. Grabbing her 'World's Best Grandmother' mug, she filled the tea ball with loose leaf Darjeeling. Her son, Jacob, had gotten her the strainer and showed her how to make tea by the cup. Not quite as good as brewing it in the pot, but far better than those nasty muslin bags full of powder pretending to be tea.

A nostalgic smile drifted across her face. Jacob had always been a fussy boy. Fastidious about his appearance. No mud pies or frogs in his pockets for him. He'd been happier with his nose in a book than playing ball with the wild, tousle-haired pack of neighborhood boys.

The smile faded. Granny tried to love her son's wife, like a good mother should, but the tart wanted a bigger life than the 'burbs of Buffalo offered and had dragged Jacob away to the West coast. She kept him and the grandkids so busy there was barely any time for a little old lady, alone in a decaying house too big for one person flanked by an overgrown lawn.

Granny huffed. Maybe she'd just give the kids a ring. She glanced at the clock. It was only five in the morning in California. She picked up the phone. One of the great things about getting old—she could pretend that she'd confused the time zones. She might wake them, but at least she could guarantee they'd be at home, not off at football practice or dance classes or the million other things that kept young people bustling here and there.

She pressed *speed dial one* and waited for the phone to ring. Instead, a tinny voice droned in her ear, "We're sorry. All circuits are busy. Please try your call again later."

She grumbled as she replaced the receiver. So much for modern technology making life easier. She'd figured out email and texting and social media ages ago (she was old, not stupid). It was all supposed to connect her to the world at the touch of a button. So how come she felt more isolated than ever?

With a sigh, she sat down to her breakfast. The egg was cold and the tea over brewed. She ate it anyway. Living on a fixed income, she couldn't afford to be wasteful.

After clearing away the dishes, she flicked on the television. It was too early in the day for her stories, but there was usually some interesting cooking show to watch. She especially liked those two stout ladies on the BBC who made everything with lard. Granny tuned in, not for the recipes—everyone knew that English food was terribly bland—but because those old broads were sassy. They didn't wait around, hoping someone would call or visit. No, they hopped on their motorcycle, sidecar and all, and toured the countryside.

Granny smirked. Ah, to be a young whippersnapper in her seventies again.

She flipped through the channels. News. News. News. Every station was playing some special report. Granny glanced around for her glasses before remembering they were on a chain around her neck. Another thoughtful gift from Jacob. A visit would be nicer, though. She shrugged, perched the glasses on the bridge of her nose, and narrowed her eyes at the broadcast.

"...appeared in the sky shortly after daybreak this morning. At this time, there has been no contact with the spaceship, but..."

Granny shook her head. Her hearing aid must be on the fritz. Spaceship? She turned up the volume on the TV.

"...extraterrestrials appear hostile in nature, as some sort of energy beam has shot all investigatory missions down. I repeat: Earth is under attack!"

Granny rolled her eyes and clicked the remote. The screen went dark. Another one of those ridiculous, sensational hoaxes. She never had much patience for science fiction. Alfred, now, he had loved a good space opera. What was that one with the robots and the big hairy wooshie? Her eyes prickled as she glanced at his threadbare recliner. Three years empty, and she still wasn't cried out. Silly old fool.

Sniffling, she headed to the bathroom to double check her hair in the mirror. Sundays at nine-thirty, the church's meal delivery people arrived with their casseroles and crocks of soup. Granny felt bad for taking the food. The chest freezer in the basement was stuffed with prepared meals she had no appetite to eat. Still, she looked forward to the delivery every week. It was nice to have a visitor. Even if they never stayed more than a minute or two.

Everyone was so busy these days.

Satisfied she looked her best, be it wrinkled and skinny, she went into the parlor to wait. And wait. She frowned. They'd never been late before. Perhaps she had the time wrong. Granny checked the schedule. Nine-thirty on Sundays, just like she thought. She was old and a tad hard of hearing, not senile.

Grouchy, she stood up to go check the front step. Maybe they were in a hurry and just left it there? As she opened the door, the chain rattled against the frame; she never used it anymore. She had nothing to steal, and navigating the hook was a challenge with her rheumatism.

No delivery.

Granny turned to go back inside, then paused. The hairs on the back of her neck stood on end. She looked up and down the street. Even for a Sunday, it seemed too quiet. No traffic. None of the neighborhood kids riding their bikes. Even Mrs. Gladstone's pampered Shih Tzu had stopped its never-ending barking.

Just as she was about to go back inside, something on the sidewalk caught her eye. An odd shimmering form, like a mirage, hovered between the mailbox and the weed-choked green strip. Granny pushed her glasses up her nose and watched, curiosity getting the best of her.

The mirage solidified into a gray-faced man with enormous round eyes. His limbs seemed too long for his body, like over-stretched elastic.

She blinked. Where the heck had he come from?

The stranger pressed a fancy device on his wrist and spoke in a rapid-fire string of clicks and whistles. For the second time that day, Granny wondered if her hearing aids needed fixing. Maybe it was time to change the battery. She clucked her tongue.

As if drawn to the noise, the man turned and fixed his gaze on her. Oversized eyes whirled as he studied her.

"Halloo, there young man!" Granny waved. "Come over here, mister. Don't you know it's impolite to stare?"

The man flickered and reappeared in front of her.

"HallOO there. ImPOlite to stare." He cocked his head as he repeated the words, putting emphasis in odd places.

"Are you lost, dearie?" Granny was certain the young man was an out-of-towner, based on his strange coveralls. "Are you here visiting someone? I'm not sure they're home."

She gestured at the neighbors' empty driveways.

"Yes, visiting. Assimilating." His voice sounded clipped, the words rattling out in a mechanical staccato.

Ah, not just an out-of-towner, but a foreigner at that.

"Well, as I said, no one's home. Why don't you come inside, and I'll fix you a cup of tea while you wait."

Not taking no for an answer, Granny hooked the man by the arm and bustled him into the house. His skin felt scaly under her fingertips.

"You know, dear. I have an excellent eczema lotion that just works wonders. You should definitely give it a try." She patted his forearm.

The man opened his mouth. "Take me to your lea—"

"Come into the kitchen, sweetheart, and I'll put on the kettle, then you can tell me all about it."

Granny pushed him into the chair at the head of the table. A twang went through her. Alfred used to read his newspaper there every morning. She shook off the memory, determined to be a good host. In an odd way, the visitor reminded her of her late husband, both bald as a ping-pong ball.

She bustled around, measuring dried leaves into her favorite blue willow teapot. Only the best for visitors. With a glance at the man's ashen face, she added another heaping spoonful of tea.

"A nice cup of English breakfast will fix you right up." At least the English did tea right.

Granny kept up a stream of chatter as the leaves steeped. She arranged a few cookies on a plate, hoping they weren't soggy.

"You know, these used to be my son's favorite. His wife doesn't let him eat processed sugar anymore, though. I say, a few sweets now and then never hurt anybody." She offered a conspiratorial smile. "I always keep a box in the pantry for when Jacob visits."

Her smile faltered. Come to think of it, they probably were stale.

The man opened his mouth, showing a row of snaggly, chipped teeth. "I've come to negotiate your surren—"

"I don't want to embarrass you, my dear, but speaking of sugar, maybe you've had a little too much."

He hadn't taken a cookie, but she moved the plate out of his reach.

"I could recommend an excellent dentist. Of course, my late husband, Alfred, was even better, but he sold his practice to a nice young man decades ago."

She smiled and proudly tapped her own teeth, still bright white and even.

"All real, you know. No falsies like a lot of people my age."

Granny poured the tea and set a mug in front of the stranger.

"Here you go. Guaranteed to put a little color in your cheeks!"

He started to speak, but she made a *drink up* motion with her hands. She lifted her own mug to her lips, and he hesitantly followed suit. The warmth from the mug seeped into her fingers as she drank. The heat felt nice on her swollen joints.

The man took a swallow and started coughing, tea spraying everywhere.

Granny sprang out of her seat—as fast as an old lady could spring—her maternal instincts kicking into overdrive.

"Hands over your head!"

She grabbed his long-fingered hands and threw them into the air, thumping him on the back for good measure. He choked and wheezed.

"How dare..." Cough, hack. "Poison..." Sniffle, cough.

"I'm so sorry, sweetheart. I should have told you it was hot!" Granny mopped up the mess with a tea towel. "Jacob always used to drink too fast as well."

With a wistful smile, she went out to the living room and pulled a heavy photo album off the shelf. The man was still spluttering when she returned. She plunked the book on the table and started turning pages.

Granny prattled on, recounting stories of Jacob's first day of school, notable blizzards back before they used to shut everything down for a few flakes, and Alfred's annual fishing trip on Lake Erie.

"He never did catch anything. Honestly, between you and me, it felt like an excuse to go boating and drink beers on the water. Only a couple, mind you, Alfred was a cautious man. Never drove impaired." She shook a stern finger at her visitor.

He shifted in his seat, eyes glazed over. Granny patted him on the hand.

"Not much of a conversationalist, are you, dearie? But you're an excellent listener." She pushed the cookie plate back across the table. "Go ahead, have one."

He glanced at his undrunk cup of tea, then back at the cookies. His too-flat nose wrinkled as he pushed back his chair.

"Are you leaving so soon?" Granny pouted.

The odd man gnashed his teeth. Backing away, he kept a wary eye on the teacup as if it were a rabid cockapoo, before slipping out the front door.

Limping after him, Granny looked up and down the street. The stranger was nowhere to be seen, only a fading shimmer remained on the sidewalk. How did he keep doing that, coming and going so quickly? Must be those long legs.

With a contented sigh, she closed the door and went to tidy up the tea things. It had been so nice to have a bit of company, even if the boy had been a tad odd. Teapot tucked away and mugs washed, Granny went to lie down for a quick nap. All that conversating had taken the energy right out of her.

Sometime later, the phone rang, jerking her out of a sound sleep. She stood, knees creaking.

"I'm coming!" She shuffled out to the kitchen and grabbed the phone. "Hello? Gertrude Kerson speaking."

"Mom! Are you all right?" The voice at the end of the line sounded breathless.

"Jacob, darling! I tried calling you this morning, but the lines were acting funny. And why wouldn't I be all right?" Such a worry wart, her son.

"Don't you pay attention to the news? There was an alien spaceship hovering right over Buffalo this morning! They say we were being invaded, but then for absolutely no reason, the ship flew off. Last I heard, it was headed out of the solar system at top speed."

Granny snorted. "Oh, Jacob. Don't be silly. There's no such thing as aliens. You and your father..." She shrugged ruefully.

"Mom, I'm telling—"

"You know, darling. It's past time you brought my grandkids for a visit." She brushed cookie crumbs off the table. "Speaking of visitors, let me tell you all about the nice young man I met today."

♀

Light years away, in sector Alpha Forty-Two, Greblok tapped out their brief for the Council. The blue-green planet, third from its sun, had initially seemed full of potential. Early reports had mentioned a low-tech, low intellect, primate population that would have made an excellent slave pool.

Greblok swallowed, throat still raw from the noxious beverage. They considered, then typed in an addendum to the report.

Even elderly specimens are excessively hostile. Unceasing auditory assault combined with poison makes them highly adversarial. Not worth the effort of assimilation.

They pressed send, then entered coordinates in the nav system for a newly discovered gas giant with an avian race worth investigating. Even better, they were thought to be telepathic communicators. Greblok smiled. It would take almost a standard revolution to get there, but they could really use some quiet time.

Dream Wedding

We start dreaming about our fairy tale wedding early because we are taught that's what little girls do. Everyone fantasizes about Prince Charming striding down the aisle with his blindingly white teeth and dimpled chin, and so should we. The vision's filled with organ music and antique ivory lace—a keepsake swatch from our mother's dress. Sprays of roses and baby's breath never wilt, and doves, no butterflies, circle our head.

It's magical.

Time doesn't tarnish the dream. We periodically trot it out, polish it on our sleeve. It isn't the '90s anymore, so we upgrade from wrinkled magazine pages to a collection of Pinterest images. Everything becomes country chic—candles in mason jars and sheafs of artfully arranged dried wheat.

It's still magical.

We categorize boyfriends into two sub-groups: *Husband Material* and *Not*. The *Nots* are let down gently. Sometimes the *Husband Materials* surprise us and end up being *Nots* in disguise. Sometimes, they turn into *Husband Material* for someone else. This is infinitely worse, watching our friend have her magical day while we wear an ugly bridesmaid dress. We tell her we love the taffeta monstrosity and then escape her unbearable joyfulness by going to dance with one of the *Nots* in the bridal party.

We do not wear the dress again.

As time goes on, we begin to worry that our Prince Charming doesn't exist. Perhaps romance isn't written in the stars for us. We're destined to be an Old Maid. It doesn't matter if we're smart and have a promising career. No one cares that we sing like a lark or can do the NYT Mini Crossword in under twenty seconds. Everyone's peering side-eyed, wondering why no one loves us. We must be desperately flawed.

Lowering our standards, we call up one of the *Nots*.

He's no prince, definitely not a charmer. His teeth aren't perfectly white and there's no dimple on his chin. We tell ourselves he's not horrible, though. We overlook his toenail clippings all over the bathroom floor. Every Sunday, he plops himself on the couch, drinking beer and belching, but we tell ourselves that's not a deal breaker. We trade our theater tickets for a football jersey and make seven-layer dip. We pretend to take an interest in the things he loves.

Maybe then he'll love us, too.

Years go by. All our friends are married. We stop getting wedding invitations, and soon pink and blue envelopes with baby booties stenciled on them arrive in the mail. Prince Not still sits on the couch. We drop little hints here and there. Leave the Dream Wedding Pinterest page open on our computer for him to see.

Eventually, he'll figure it out.

It's a Tuesday night, and he's horny. We let him paw at us; it's quicker and easier than turning him away. After, we find our own release in the bathroom. We slide back into bed, and he pulls us close, half asleep. It's kind of nice, not fireworks, but warm and snuggly. If a little sweaty. In a drowsy mumble, he asks if we want to get hitched. There's no ring, no declarations of eternal love.

We say yes anyway.

Our mom tells us her wedding dress is long gone. She feels bad, but she'd given up on us getting married ages ago. It's ok, we assure her, dress shopping is part of the fun. None of our friends can go with us, though. They all have play dates and second-grade recitals to attend. We pick out the perfect bone-white sheath alone in the dressing room. It's all elegant lines and sophisticated simplicity. The cashier wraps the two-sizes-too-small gown in tissue paper.

The wedding diet begins today.

Prince Not works late on cake tasting day. We're so hangry we hang up on him and invite our bestie and her five-year-old to come with us instead. They like the triple-layer hazelnut. We think lemon chiffon is classier. Not that a single bite passes our lips. Five more pounds to go to fit into the dress. We sneak nibbles of rice cakes from our purse, and text pictures to Prince Not.

We order chocolate. His favorite.

Apparently, candles aren't allowed in the hall, and we scour craft sites to figure out what to do with all those mason jars. Country chic is out. The jars go into the recycling. We stay up all night exchanging dried wheat centerpieces for snowy canna lilies. Classics never go out of style. Desperate to salvage some part of the dream, we find a website that'll overnight us live butterflies.

Two days until the magic.

Of course, we get our period, but grit our teeth and power through. There's a zillion things left to do. Pick up the cake. Wrap the bridesmaids' gifts. Nails. Hair. Get our mom from the airport. Write checks for the DJ and the caterer. Double-check the seating chart. Who put Uncle Dom next to his third ex-wife? Everything will have to be rearranged. In between errands, we swing by the drugstore for tampons and Midol. There's no time for cramps or bloating.

We make our husband-to-be a list—get a haircut, pick up tux.

The ceremony is...fine. Totally fine. Sure, the flower girl dumps all the petals in a pile and then hides under a pew. No big deal that the pastor fast-talks and no one understands a word. Not a catastrophe that an early frost killed all the butterflies, so our family throws rice like a bunch of heathens. We're married. That's all that matters. The reception starts, and the food is fantastic. As buffets go.

We catch Prince Not ogling a bridesmaid.

He never got his hair cut either. Ironically, it's the latter that makes us mad. He only had two fucking things on his list and couldn't even manage that. We realize he'll always be Prince *Not*. He's never once gone kayaking with us and refuses to even try sushi. He thinks theater is for "the gays." He says stupid things like "the gays." Our future is football and burritos and handling our own orgasms. For the rest of our life.

Wrapped up in the dream of a magical wedding, we forgot about the happily ever after. We should have just adopted a dog.

Finding Immortality

The Technician stepped into the room, then hesitated, shifting foot to foot with nervous energy. He looked fresh out of medical school. These days, looks were deceiving, but I'd read his file—still in his original biovessel. His hands clutched a holoboard, knuckles white, but he didn't need to read the chart to find my name.

"Good Morning, Dr. Steb—erm, Elyse."

I pasted on a reassuring smile and forgave the stutter-step in the prescribed rhetoric. To put the patients at ease, we used their given names, but he was young, and it wasn't every day one Transferred their boss's boss.

He paused, collecting himself, then carried on.

"Now, I know you might have questions, but rest assured, I'll be with you every step of the way as I help you Transfer into your new biovessel."

Straight from the corporate SOP. I should know, I'd written it, lifetimes ago.

The Technician flushed scarlet.

"Um, right. You probably know all that."

He rubbed a hand over his head, leaving his hair sticking up. A younger me would have found it endearing, back when I cared about that kind of thing. I took pity on him.

"Forget I'm Dr. Stebbings and invented all this."

I waved my hand to encompass the nursebot in its docking station, the upload panel, the patented HALO headpiece. In the race for immortality, I had discovered the next best thing—consciousness transference. Humans were no longer limited to a single lifetime in an aged, ill, or broken-down biovessel. He was right to be awed; it was spectacular. And a nightmare of my own making.

It took effort to remember to keep smiling. I didn't particularly care so much about putting the boy at ease, but I needed him to get through this and complete the upload.

"Today, I'm just old lady Elyse, looking for a respite from crippling arthritis."

The Technician's Adam's apple bobbed as he swallowed hard.

"Honestly, this is my first solo Transfer, so having you request me personally was a little nerve-wracking."

"I've heard excellent things about you from your team lead."

I patted him on the arm. The skin on the back of my hand was papery thin and crosshatched like a dried riverbed.

"Pretend you're back in the skills lab. Tell me about the tracking drug."

He rummaged in his coat pocket, clearly relieved at the change of subject.

"The tracking drug is a critical part of the process. It introduces a unique isotope that temporarily affects brain chemistry, creating distinct neural patterns."

I nodded encouragingly.

"And why is that important?"

The Technician launched into a textbook-perfect lecture.

"After we upload the consciousness, the patterns allow us to track the patient within the Ultranet and ultimately download their neurological essence into the new biovessel. Without identifiable patterns, it's impossible to distinguish the *person* from the *data*. The tracking process was developed in 2073, after—" He broke off.

"After the insufferable and arrogant Dr. Stebbings lost her beloved daughter in the data stream trying to cheat a terminal cancer diagnosis," I finished for him.

My stomach clenched. I'd spent half a dozen lifetimes trying to get her out. Without the tracker, download had proved impossible. I took a shaky breath and motioned for him to carry on.

The Technician pulled a bottle of pills from his pocket. Old-fashioned, but the slow-release format worked better than an instadermal patch to sustain the isotope-induced brain patterns. I held out my hand, and he shook the yellow orb into my waiting palm.

"Water?"

He nodded and fussed with the comestibles dispenser built into the far wall. It took a moment. I'd fiddled with the output settings before he'd arrived, and he mumbled to himself as he jabbed the buttons with increasing frustration.

I smothered a grin. Rule number one: never turn your back on your patient. I'd been counting on his naiveté.

When he finally handed me the glass, I took a sip, swallowed. Opened my mouth.

"No need, Dr.... Elyse. I trust you understand the importance of the tracker."

A steel band tightened around my chest. Poor kid was going to have a mess to deal with after.

"Best to follow protocol."

He nodded and reluctantly ensured I hadn't tucked the pill in my cheek. Not that any normal person would, but after the *incident*, I'd written checks and double checks into the operating procedures so no one else would lose their loved one in the data stream. My fists curled in the bedsheets.

It only took a few minutes for the Technician to fit the HALO device over my temples and trigger the initiation sequence.

"While the upload gets started, I'm just going to zip down to the lab and bring your Transfer vessel up. The new bioprinted models are really quite exquisite. You'll be out riding a magbike in no time!"

I nodded, feigning interest.

He pressed a button, and the nursebot hummed to life.

"Nurse Nelly, here, will keep me updated on your progress."

My limbs grew heavy. Static washed over my mind in a gentle rhythm. It surged and retreated, pulling pieces of me with it like waves sucking the sand from beneath my feet at the shore.

♀

In a vast, satin ocean, synapses fire lightning-bright in the never-ending now. Neurons float like luminescent jellyfish in the infinite darkness. One by one, the threads connecting me to my biovessel sever. Muscles relax and a fist uncurls. I can almost feel the little yellow pill falling from where it is hidden in my palm. What used to be my palm.

I drift above the seascape like dandelion seeds—once part of a whole, now a cloud of individual thoughts floating on the wind. There's no direction, even so, I move. With superhuman effort, I force the bits of fluff together and transform into a pelican, wings stretched impossibly wide as I soar over the onyx sea. Searching.

Hours. Days. Years. Decades. Nanoseconds. There's only the search. What? Who? I'm certain I'll know when I find it. Them. Her?

Below, the jellyfish swarm together, becoming an elegant sailfish, blue and green scales sparkling jewel-like against the India ink waves. She races below. I chase after her, but she's unspeakably fast. My muscles strain as I try to keep up, but the harder I flap, the slower I fly. I'm not sure I understand the rules of this place.

Storm clouds appear, angry gray cotton candy that sucks me into a swirling vortex. Rouge data batters me like diamond-sharp hail. I lose sight of the marlin as I fight the raging gale on tattered wings. Feathers strip away, fragments of my soul scattering. I can feel thoughts and memories slipping away.

Accepting the Excellence in Neuro-Innovation Award.

Sour-sweet berries bursting on my tongue.

Dancing at a low-grav soiree.

The shock of a positive pregnancy test.

Cozy blankets, straight from the dryer.

Piece by piece, it's all ripped away, thousands of disjointed bytes caught in the data stream's wild current.

A small voice calling, "Momma!" I shake my head. That's not a memory; it's here.

Will. Intention. I finally understand the rules.

I scatter the tempest with a thought. My glossy wings catch an updraft. Below, the ocean surges in towering waves as I search for a glimpse of the sailfish's pointed bill. A pattern of syncopated flashes draws my attention like blinking fireflies on a moonless night.

Laughter fills the light-dappled darkness. Mine or hers?

I tuck my wings and dive. Just as I hit the water, the sailfish leaps. Her shadow crosses over me as I plunge below the breakers. I surface. Shoot into the air. She splashes back down. We weave a figure eight.

Dive. Leap. Dive. Leap. For a lifetime, we dance.

In the distance, a klaxon sounds. Panicked voices. *...didn't take the tracker...upload nearly complete...we'll lose her...*

Water drips from my wings. I flap twice and rise into the air. No one is lost. I watch as the sailfish cuts through the waves. She circles around the jellyfish, herding them into intricate patterns.

Someone is found. We both are.

A final thread snaps and a weight falls away, freeing me from the biovessel that binds me to physical reality. There's no going back. Why would I want to? This is true immortality.

Below, more jellyfish coalesce into white sand. Palm trees spread their verdant fingers in the salt-kissed breeze. The sailfish floats onto the beach, tail becoming legs. She looks up. Smiles.

"Momma! Let's build a sandcastle!"

I circle once around the island, then land. The sand is warm beneath my bare feet. I glance down and the grains become piles of ones and zeros. I blink and the data stream reverts to a sun-drenched beach.

Concentrating, I twist the code. A bucket and pail materialize in my hand. They feel solid—as real as the island and the sea. I grin. Eternity in the Ultranet has so much potential and I can't wait to explore. Later. Right now, my daughter wants to build a sandcastle.

Unseen

I was fading from the mirror.

Nearly imperceptible at first, my hair seemed drab, skin sallow. I tried dyes—the kind that promised they could cover even the stubbornest of grays. An hour in rubber gloves with the scent of chemicals singeing my nose, and my once raven locks still seemed lackluster. Not threaded with strands of age-earned silver, but like a child's drawing whose unpracticed hand pressed too lightly with the crayon.

I had no more luck with makeup. Disappointed with a natural bronze, I moved to shades more vivid, even lurid. Crimson lips, smoky eyes, and winged liner so deep if I blinked too hard, I might have taken flight. Nothing worked. I resembled a washed-out photograph, bleached by the sun.

As things worsened, I feared going out in public, certain I'd be fixed with incredulous stares. I expected comments like, *oh Sasha, you look so pale. Are you feeling alright?* They never came. Everyone just looked the other way, and I chalked their silence up to well-bred manners. If you have nothing nice to contribute, then say nothing and all those other tired cliches. The alternative—that they didn't see—left a hard-to-swallow lump in my throat.

This morning, my edges softened, becoming hazy. Perhaps I needed glasses. No. Everything else appeared sharp and clear. Only I seemed indistinct, my edges bleeding into the background. I fought back a rising feeling of unease. Surely someone would notice this and validate me.

Too unnerved to eat breakfast, I sipped weak tea and sorted through yesterday's mail. Hidden amongst a stack of junk addressed to "resident," I found a card-sized envelope. I grimaced as I recognized the blocky handwriting. Tearing it open, I stared at an invitation to my brother's Jack-and-Jill. The party was tomorrow, as if including me was an afterthought.

My stomach lurched, and I dumped the rest of the tea down the sink. The thought of spending an afternoon listening to my mother nattering on about my sibling's recent accomplishments. *Your brother did this, and oh my gosh, that,* made my head pound. I tried to remember the last time Mom had asked about my work, my life. Or when she'd last called.

Needing to shake off my jitters, I walked to the office. It was easy to drift alone in the crowd, a dry leaf swept down the sidewalk in a rushing stream of commuters. I dodged between men in smart sport coats, too engrossed in their cell phones to step aside for me. A briefcase cracked against my legs, but its owner didn't glance up from his screen, let alone apologize. It stung. Part of me drank in the pain, relieved to feel solid.

Arriving at work, I shaded my eyes as sunlight sparkled off the glass and steel high rise. Envious of the sun's brilliance, I crossed the lot, sensible heels clacking on pavement. A flashy convertible—one of the guys in marketing—occupied my parking space. Again. I wanted to march up to his spacious corner office and give him a piece of my mind.

Who do you think you are, Mr. Fancy Pants?

I huffed at the silly fantasy. No one liked women who made a fuss. I had walked; I didn't need the spot for my conservative sedan today. Unconvinced by my own rationale, I shook off the thought and stepped inside.

It took a moment for my eyes to adjust to the dim lobby. The chill flow of the air conditioner washed over me, and I rubbed my battered knees while I waited for the elevator. It seemed to take forever, the little yellow light stuck up on the fifth floor.

Bing!

A lively group brushed by as the burnished steel doors slid open. Someone stepped on my toes. My coworkers filed in, chatting and laughing, rehashing last night's game, joking about a bad blind date. A flock of magpies, bound by nonchalant camaraderie. None of the birds chirped hello or made space for me. I gripped my purse strap with white knuckles but bit my tongue as I stood by to wait for the next elevator.

Once upstairs, I made my way down the hall toward my cramped cubicle. An analyst harrumphed and pushed past me, as if I were too slow or took up too much space. His elbow caught on my bag, yanking it off my shoulder. The designer knockoff vomited its contents across the carpet.

"Excuse me, Sarah."

Sarah?

At least it tickled the ear in a similar way as 'Sasha.' Last week my supervisor had called me 'Amy' and when I didn't respond, she'd laid on the passive-aggressive guilt like marmalade on toast. She'd stalked away before I could loosen my tongue and stammer an undeserved apology.

Without making eye contact, the analyst continued on his way, stomping in irritation, as if I was the one at fault. Face burning, I stuffed tampons, a half-empty tin of breath mints, and some spare change back in my purse.

A mid-morning meeting found me passing around a stack of glossy files to a room full of well-pressed suits. My pulse spiked, but before I could begin the presentation, the department head congratulated Evan on the new financial roll out.

Hey! That was my idea.

Flustered, I raised a hand in protest. No one noticed over a chorus of compliments and jostling elbows, all eager to be the first to clap the man with the stolen proposal on the back. I slunk out of the room and hid in the bathroom until I was certain the meeting had ended. No one commented on my absence or my smeared mascara.

By afternoon my stomach rumbled, and I pulled out a paper sack to eat lunch at my desk. Egg salad seasoned with spreadsheets. I used to stretch my legs and walk down to the cafeteria, but it felt awkward eating on my own. Not for being alone exactly, but for no one noticing I was alone. No one shot covert glances towards my solitary corner table; no one hid giggles behind their hands as they sniped at my expense.

How had I gotten here, where pity would have been some pittance of recognition?

If I were more daring, I'd waltz in and plonk down at a table. Not a crowded one, maybe with two or three people. *Lovely weather we're having today,* I'd say. *What did you think of Evan's proposal?* I'd lean in conspiratorially. *Funny, it seemed far more original when I came up with that plan a week ago!* They'd be indignant on my behalf and tell me I should report him. Then they'd ask me to join them again next week.

Glaring at the slow-moving clock, I tossed my empty lunch bag in the trash and wished the day away, more out of habit than desire. I had nowhere important to be after work.

I took the long way home. Twilight wrapped the city in countless shades of purple, and one by one, the lights blinked on. Warm squares of yellow spilled across the sidewalk and animated conversations poured from crowded bars and restaurants. I lingered on the outskirts of the cozy, friendly hubbub.

Peering into a noisy pub, I watched a table of women around my age. Colorful dresses, bold jewelry, silky manes of auburn and golden hair turned them into a rainbow-hued garden of bright flowers. They laughed and clinked glasses.

I imagined marching through the door, chin up and a wide smile. I'd laugh, *TGIF ladies!* They'd turn and shout my name, beckoning me over and clamoring for my attention. *Sit here, Sasha! No, here next to me!*

I deflated, a balloon with a slow leak, as one of the women glanced out the window and looked straight through me. I turned and shuffled on.

When I arrived home, I locked up behind me, threw the deadbolt and fastened the chain. Safety was an ingrained routine, though I lived in a quiet, middle-class neighborhood. I'd never had trouble. I couldn't recall the last time someone had come to the door. Even the delivery man would abandon my online shopping on the cheery welcome mat, certain I wasn't home.

I hung my purse on its hook, slipped off my shoes and arranged them neatly beside their fellows. For a moment, I hesitated, plagued by a feeling of something out of place. Spice jars lined the counter like a squadron of soldiers—cardamom, cumin, chili powder—labels facing forward in a precise row. Unread fashion magazines stacked neatly on the coffee table. Their glossy covers offered advice on how to catch a man and what style jeans would flatter every figure. Bills, organized by 'paid' and 'unpaid,' filled the wire file on the desk. Two chairs, the one I sat in and the one with the cushion fluffed like new, remained tucked squarely under the kitchen table. Everything seemed to be in its proper place.

Still, I couldn't shake the feeling. I scrubbed sweaty hands on my skirt, then fished my phone out of my pocket.

One missed call.

A spark of excitement fluttered through me as I pressed play. I could feel a goofy grin stretch my mouth, imagining a coworker inviting me to drinks or a neighbor that hoped I'd attend a weekend bar-b-que. *Oh Sasha, you just have to come! It wouldn't be the same without you!* Or perhaps it would be my brother, *hey Sashy-girl! So sorry your invitation to my Jack-and-Jill got delayed. I put the wrong amount of postage on and it got returned. I hope you can fit it into your schedule!*

My face fell, and the fantasies died. In the background, a tinny voice offered a spectacular, one-time opportunity to renew my car's warranty. The message continued, unaware of my disappointment. Sighing, I moved to press the delete button and silence the noise.

I froze.

As my hand hovered over the screen, the backlight illuminated my fingers. The perky telemarketer blathered on, but the words didn't register as I stared through my splayed palm. Icy sweat slicked down my spine. I stood rooted to the carpet, trying to make sense of what I saw.

Wrenching my feet up, I dashed into the bathroom and snapped on the light. I choked back a strangled yelp when I saw my reflection. The face in the mirror was an eerie, diaphanous specter. She had my wavy hair, the familiar scar on my chin. She even wore my favorite wrap skirt, yet I could see the room behind her ghostly image, reflected in stark relief.

I brought a trembling hand up to my face, half expecting it to pass right through. Flesh met flesh, and I sagged against the sink. Still solid, if oddly transparent, like faintly colored cellophane. Fascinated, like gawking at a train wreck, I peered through my chest. Behind me, jewel-toned fish swam on the plastic shower curtain. I shifted, and the school wavered, as if I watched them through the thick glass of an aquarium.

A giggle bubbled from my throat at the absurdity. The chuckle grew to a raucous cackle. I fell to my knees, shaking. Eyes squeezed shut as the laughter transitioned to body wracking sobs. I slumped over, curled in a ball on the cool tile.

My mother's voice scolded in my head.

No one likes a crybaby, Sasha. Why can't you be more like your brother?

Scrubbing my hand over my wet cheeks, I took a shuddering breath. My arms felt like lead, feet heavy as stone. The weight of inevitability crushed my chest, and I stared up at the ceiling.

Would anyone notice when I truly disappeared?

Inventory of Mom's Attic

- Boxes of clothes, labeled by decade in black Sharpie: 70s, 80s, 90s. (You had such elegant penmanship, Mom.) Drop off at thrift store.
- Multiple sewing machines, broken and scavenged for parts. Trash. (Note to self: before donating clothes, look for that green dress you made me. Everything comes back in fashion.)
- Grandma's Wedgwood china. Dusty, but serviceable. (You hated it; called it "fussy.") Set aside for Cousin Beth.
- Holiday decor. Not worth trying to untangle the string lights. Trash. Keep the satin ornaments you brought back from Japan. (Would it even be Christmas without them?)
- One tattered ragdoll you said "got lost" on that vacation we took to Florida right before Dad left. Keep. (Ew. No, it reeks of mothballs and Coppertone.) Trash.
- Old sketchbooks. Some of these are good. (You never mentioned you were an artist.)
- Love letters? Years of them, through early '75, shortly before you had me. (Ask Aunt Maria who Jason is. Damn, these are steamy! Did Dad know?)
- Books: Nietzsche, Thoreau, Homer, Márquez. (I thought you only read Nora Roberts. It's like I never even knew you.)
- Kid toys. Donate. (I don't remember any of these. They're all brand new. Why didn't you give them to me?)
- Unopened cards addressed to me? *Happy bday, Polly. Luv Dad. Merry Xmas, kiddo. Luv Dad. Happy graduation! So proud. Luv, Dad.* (That's not Dad's handwriting. WTF?)
- So, many papers. Bank statements, old report cards, newspaper clippings. (A paternity test? Who the fuck is Jason, Mom?) For that matter, who the hell am I?

To Join a Brotherhood

Inge woke, her heart fluttering.

Peaceful sounds drifted through the longhouse. A swaddled toddler cooed in his sleep, and someone grunted before rolling over to snuggle deeper into their pallet. The familiar scents of smoke, honey mead, and warm bodies filled the air. Everything appeared as it should.

Hvat? Strange.

Drawn by an unseen force, Inge slipped from beneath a layer of thick sleeping furs. Cold nipped at her as she tiptoed across the hard-packed dirt floor. She paused when her favored kinsman, Hjálmarr, snorted and edged closer to the glowing embers of a dying fire. After he settled, she bent over and slipped her bare feet into his oversized boots. She knew the grizzled berserkir wouldn't mind.

A silent echo called to her in the voice of the divine. Outside. Inge went. One such as she did not question the will of the gods.

Beyond the shelter of the longhouse, the wind whispered a promise of snow as it threaded icy fingers through her hair. Already the mountains were capped in white. By day, ornery brown bears foraged in the woods, preparing for their long winter sleep. In the dark, small creatures skittered through the underbrush, desperately squirreling away food stores. Both man and beast grew tense on the cusp of the changing season. Winter was cruel in Noregr.

A buzz of anticipation rattled Inge's bones. She breathed deeply, letting the crisp air clear the dregs of sleep from her head. A gust tossed fallen leaves in a miniature cyclone at her feet, then sped off to chase puffy woolen clouds across the dark sky. As the clouds cleared, Máni, the moon god, appeared and cast a river of silver over the ground.

Inge's skin pebbled with gooseflesh. Something wild and savage lurked in the tree line. She turned to see a hulking shape disentangle from the shadows, its fur darker than raven wings. Unblinking eyes fastened on her. They reflected gold in the moonlight.

Inge froze. The wind died, and the forest held its breath.

Úlfr.

The wolf padded forward on silent paws. It tested the air. With deadly grace, it circled the young woman. Inge swallowed but held her ground. Úlfr were sacred. The beast drew closer. She could feel its hot breath against her skin. Dagger-sharp fangs glistened. Its hackles raised, and a low growl rumbled deep in its chest.

Hail Odin, one-eyed All Father, find me worthy.

The wolf bowed its head, a wary greeting between new allies, and a thrill ran through Inge.

Overhead, a cloud obscured the moon. When it reappeared, the wolf was gone, melted into the night as if it had been naught but a dream.

No, a sign.

Ulfheðinn, the All Father's elite wolf warriors, were chosen, not made.

Inge threw her head back and howled.

♀

Hjálmarr's breath puffed white.

"You don't have to do this, píka." His face flushed pink in the cold, making the pale scar running across his cheek stand out in contrast.

"Don't call me 'girl.' I'm a grown woman." Inge snorted. "And I must do this. Odin chose me to join the Ulfheðinn Brotherhood. There is no denying the All Father."

"*Bróðir*, not *systir*. There has never been a woman ulfheðinn."

Inge frowned but didn't answer. She picked her way up the rocky mountain trail. A loose stone turned underfoot, and she stutter-stepped in order to avoid twisting an ankle.

Hjálmarr would love an excuse to put a halt to this, the big oaf.

The thought held no bite. She knew the ulfheðinn worried for her. Many attempted the Trial, but few survived to wear the sacred wolf skin. Her stomach roiled. After her brother failed, there hadn't been enough of him left for the funeral pyre. The vacant look on their mother's face haunted Inge's dreams.

I am not my bróðir. I was chosen. I will make our móðir proud.

As the pair climbed, the sun sank below the rocky summit, and shadows painted a violet gloaming. Inge pushed herself to keep up with the burly warrior's longer strides. Her thighs burned, but she did not complain. The great goddess Hel would drag Inge to the underworld before she showed weakness.

Inge picked up the pace, jabbing Hjálmarr with an elbow as she passed him by.

"Say your piece, frændi. I know you well enough to tell when you are chewing on your thoughts. You look as if you've bitten into a pear only to find half a worm."

The older man huffed.

"I didn't teach you the ways of battle to watch you die in the Trial." Hjálmarr hitched his snowy wolf skin cloak closer around his shoulders. The rare white pelt marked him first among equals in the brotherhood. "You fight with the wrath of a cornered badger, even without the berserkir's bog myrtle. You could be the greatest Shield Maiden that ever lived. Konungr Harold Hárfagri would welcome your service."

"And I will fight for the fair-haired king." Inge bared her teeth. "As ulfheðinn. There was a sign."

"A sign no one but you saw!" Hjálmarr's voice rose to an angry shout.

"Do you doubt me?" Hurt crept in like hoarfrost on Wintersnight. Inge forced a levity in her tone she didn't feel. "Have I ever spoken false, you old goat?"

Hjálmarr roared.

"Old?" He spun, sweeping Inge's legs out from under her.

Inge fell backward. She bit back a curse and grabbed the ulfheðinn's tunic. Using his momentum against him, she pulled him down with her. They rolled, each scrabbling to come out on top. Inge twisted like a forest cat, forcing Hjálmarr onto his back. He bucked once, then stilled.

Inge pressed the blade of her hunting knife to his throat.

"Call me a liar again, and I'll shave off that scraggly sheep's hide you call a beard."

Hjálmarr chuckled.

"Perhaps, Odin willing, you just might survive the Trial." He pushed her off and rose to his feet with warrior's grace. "That was a clever trick."

"The wolf is smaller than the bear and so uses speed and wiles to take down her opponent."

You taught me that.

She didn't say it aloud, but her mentor smiled as if she had.

♀

A score of ulfheðinn gathered in the darkness on the stark plateau. They huddled together in twos and threes, grumbling and casting scornful glances at Inge. She glowered and set her shoulders, spine rigid as an old oak.

How dare they?

Hjálmarr cleared his throat.

"Brothers, I bring before you Inge, daughter of Sven Helvig, our honored Jarl." He turned and faced Inge, eyes flashing. "Shield Maiden, will you heed the call of the gods and enter into the Wolf Trial?"

Inge nodded, unable to find her voice.

The mutters intensified.

...chieftain's daughter...

...women are not berserkir, undeserving the mark of the wolf...

...she'll ne'r survive the bear...

Anger flared at their words, and Inge clenched her fists. Who were they to deny the All Father's mandate?

"Enough!" Hjálmarr's voice ricocheted off the mountainside. "Odin has marked her as favored. She will be allowed to attempt the Trial."

Silence fell. Norsemen respected omens. Inge smiled. They respected Hjálmarr even more. Many of the brotherhood owed their lives to the powerful berserkir.

Someone handed Inge a horn.

"Drink."

She took a deep draught and spluttered. Fermented bog myrtle curdled on her tongue. Hjálmarr gave her a hard look, and she downed the rest of the sour brew.

He nodded once, then pulled his fur cloak close. The white pelt shone strangely bright in the starlit night.

"The wolf's strength is fearlessness."

Hjálmarr helped Inge out of her boots. She shed her tunic and trousers and left them in a pile like discarded snakeskin. The wolf wore no armor, nor would she.

I should feel cold.

Her bare skin tingled as the bog myrtle sent a wave of heat through her. She curled her lip and growled.

Her mentor pressed a simple bone knife into her hand.

Claw and fang.

The thought felt fuzzy, the words fading, shifting to more visceral images and sensations as the bog myrtle did its work.

Hjálmarr bowed, and more images, memories, flashed across her mind's eye.

Two cubs wrestling in a spring meadow under their frændi's watchful eye.

Her bróðir was no match for her speed.

The white wolf laughed and cheered them on.

Crooked teeth, as her bróðir grinned and waved, off to face the Trial.

An empty funeral pyre. She stood beside their móðir, feeling the heat on her face, and made a vow to redeem the family name.

The white wolf nuzzled her shoulder, bringing her back to the present. He smelled of approval and pride. A thread of fear. Regret. Acceptance. Inge growled and pushed him off. She was ready.

One by one, the ulfheðinn stepped into the shadows. Gray and brown fur flowed over their shoulders. They pulled their hoods up—leathered snouts and ears, turning warriors into uncanny beast men.

Spears rattled against shields like drums. Heartbeats.

An ember flared in Inge's stomach. She shifted the bone dagger from hand to hand as the spark grew into a gnawing hunger. The rage became a need to bite and claw. To rend flesh.

Time shifted, past and future dropping away. There was only now within the battle fury.

The berserkir frenzy swelled, and Inge lunged at the shadows. Beast men sidestepped. Their shield wall forced her back into the center of the circle. She snapped her teeth. Her pulse thrummed, blood boiling.

Something snuffled.

Musk filled Inge's nose as the bear lumbered into the clearing. A rumble built deep in her throat. The bear peeled its lips back, snarling in reply. It clawed the ground, gouging deep furrows in the dirt.

The circle of ulfheðinn whispered and swayed. Flashes of fur and fang, spears and shields, two legs. Four. Inge shook her head and turned her back on the wolf men. The brotherhood wouldn't interfere—the Trial was for her alone to win. Or to die.

Rising on its hind legs, the bear roared. It swiped at her with surprising swiftness. Claws flashed. Three red lines tore across Inge's chest. She leapt back.

The watchers bayed. First blood. Rage guided Inge's knife, and the fight began in earnest.

Spin. Leap. Snap. Grapple. Slash.

Blood dripped down Inge's face, but she felt no pain.

Spears drummed on shields like thunder. Tooth and claw and bunched muscles; deadly grace and brute strength. Wolf and bear. Blood dripped where fangs tore at soft flesh.

A whimper. A scream.

Thought fled, and the battle fury took control.

♀

Inge woke, an unknown eternity later, with a furred boulder crushing her chest and daggers buried in her shoulder. Groaning, she wriggled out from beneath the weight. Even with her bone knife buried deep in the bear's sightless eye, the beast left a final score as its claws ripped from her flesh. She moaned. The air in her lungs felt like splinters, and for a time, she did nothing but try to breathe.

The battle fury had faded, leaving Inge hollow. Her tongue tasted of blood and sour myrtle. The aftereffects of the drug left reality fractured.

Am I dauðr?

She flexed aching muscles. Not dead, then.

The night writhed. A wolf pack circled, drew closer.

Inge shook her head. Wolves became men in furred cloaks. She struggled to her feet and pulled the dagger from the bear's still-warm corpse, then turned to stare at them defiantly. The cold night air puckered her bare skin.

Hjálmarr stepped forward and wrapped her in a wolf hide, blacker than raven wings. The fur felt silky and warm. For a moment, Inge thought she saw golden eyes in the darkness. When she blinked, they were gone.

Thank you, systir úlfr.

A heavy hand landed on her shoulder, and she gritted her teeth but didn't flinch.

"Welcome to the Ulfheðinn Brotherhood."

Inge smirked. "Bróðir? I think we're going to need a new name."

All around her, the ulfheðinn threw back their heads and howled.

Repainting Eden

Εὐρυνόμη trails her fingers over the paint tubes. Navy, cobalt, lapis lazuli. So many shades of blue. She takes her time. It's critical to choose the perfect hue.

With practiced hands, the goddess makes her selection and unscrews the cap. She picks up a wide-bristle brush; finer details can be added later. On a backdrop of nothingness, she layers swaths of bright, cerulean blue. The sky is reborn.

"Stop fidgeting, Lilith." Father aimed his words in my direction but looked through me.

I froze, like a spotlighted deer. Maybe if I improved my posture, got straight As, looked perfect, he'd be proud of me. Father turned away, and I vowed to be better. Then he'd see me.

Ultramarine and sea foam separate the blue sky from the blue ocean. Εὐρυνόμη paints waves and currents and tides. Dabs of titanium white form cotton-ball clouds. She leans forward and her breath becomes a salt-kissed breeze that chases the fluff across the heavens.

"You should smile more, Lil." He stood too close, edging me back against the wall.

I tried to protest, to say no, but his mouth crashed onto mine, stealing the words. His hands were rough, fingers digging into my thighs. I struggled, but my arms felt like noodles pushing against a boulder. It hurt less if I remained still.

Gloria Gaynor's "I Will Survive" looped in my head. I concentrated on the lyrics, pretending it was true, and waited for him to be done.

The color wheel holds as many greens as blues. The softness of new grasses and the vibrant emerald treetops. Seaweed and cactuses. Frogs and dragonfly wings. Mint, limes, celery, pears. Εὐρυνόμη paints them all.

Land grows next to the sea—rich brown soil and a rainbow of flowers. What Chaos destroyed, she creates anew.

"Should we go to the Chinese buffet for lunch?" He elbowed his friend and scoffed. "Just don't tell Fat Linda in Sales. It's all-you-can-eat, and she'd wipe them out!"

I shrank back into my office to eat a limp salad at my desk. The older I got, the harder it was to lose weight. Diets, calorie counting, hours at the gym. None of it worked. I couldn't decide if being called fat was worse than them not knowing my name after working together for years.

"Fuck them." I swept the salad into the trash and sat down to type my resignation.

Εὐρυνόμη studies what she's made. A perfect replica of old Earth. Better. No pollution, no hatred, no war. She frowns. It's missing something.

She reaches into the void, rifling through the shadows. Chaos pushes back, unwilling to let a prize go, but Εὐρυνόμη is determined. She tugs a battered, faded spirit free. It sparks defiantly in her hand.

Perfect.

She paints flesh on the soul and frees it into the new world.

Lilacs and petrichor scented the air. The universe felt freshly painted, and I was chosen to be the reincarnation of Eve.

"Why me?"

Εὐρυνόμη spoke in my head. ***Because you're a fighter, Lilith.***

I nodded. Perhaps this time, I could do more than just survive.

A Lifetime of Moments

Moira dials the number he gave her. The line seems dead. No beeping, no ringing—how can there be? Still, she waits. He'll know she wants to talk. She doesn't know how it works; it just does. No point dwelling on mechanics.

"Hello, sweetheart."

A warmth fills her chest. Sometimes, he's too busy working to answer. She closes her eyes and tries not to think about that. He's on the other end of the line now and that's all that matters. She fights a tickle in her throat and musters a playful, conspiratorial tone.

"I'm calling to RSVP for *you-know-what*." Her thudding heartbeats fill the silence as she waits for him to respond.

"You know that's not how it works."

She huffs, but her breath catches and turns into a hacking cough. When it subsides, she wipes phlegm from her lips, ignoring the crimson smear on the back of her hand.

"We both know my name's in the Book. Everyone's is." Moira sucks in a wheezy breath. "Just whisper the date and time in my ear."

"Why are you in such a rush?"

"Why aren't you?" She can't hide her disappointment.

Again, the silence stretches between them, spun sugar and just as fragile. When he speaks, his voice trembles.

"There's so much you don't understand."

Moira doesn't ask him to explain. If he hasn't by now, he never will.

NINE

Lining her feet up at the edge of the water, Moira clutched a stone in her chubby grip and whipped it across the pond's glassy surface.

Ker-PLUNK!

"Gramps! I can't do it." Face scrunched, she pouted.

Her grandfather grunted but didn't look up from his fishing pole. She grinned. A grunt from Gramps was better than *keep it up!* from anyone else. She turned to look for another rock and stopped.

A strange boy with dimpled cheeks and wild, dark curls stood a few paces away.

"Who are you?" Moira took a step back, her sneakers sinking in the mud. Chilly water soaked the bell-bottoms of her jeans.

He jumped, as if surprised she'd noticed him. His eyes were like the sky; she could lie on her back and stare into the pretty blue. Or maybe they were green like the snap peas in Mom's garden—no, shiny, like beetle wings. Now brown as Tootsie Rolls. Perhaps smoke-gray like the kittens born in the hayloft last week?

The boy shook his head, and the rainbow-spell broke.

"Here. Flat ones skip best."

He offered a smooth oval stone. His skin felt cold against hers as he showed her how to hold her fingers and flick her wrist.

"One...two...three!" Moira squealed as the rock skipped over the surface of the water, then disappeared, leaving only rippling circles behind. "I did it!"

She pranced around the boy, pumping her fists, his oddness forgiven in her excitement. He watched her, an uncertain smile curling his lips as if he wanted to laugh along but wasn't sure it was allowed.

"Gramps! Did you see?"

Her grandfather didn't move. His hand dangled over the arm of his folding chair. A puddle from an overturned beer can spread on the weathered dock.

"Gramps?" Moira's skin prickled as if a parade of ants marched up her arms.

The boy pointed towards the house.

"Go get your mom."

The wind stilled. Ripples on the pond froze. Everything stopped as if she and the boy had sidestepped time. Moira hugged her arms around herself. She blinked, and the boy disappeared. When she looked again, he hovered behind her grandfather's chair.

Flat black eyes met her gaze. "Go."

The world restarted, and Moira ran. Not because he said so, but to escape the sadness in his voice.

♀

Moira plucks at the bedsheets. "You could have told me back then what was happening."

Though she can't see his expression, she predicts his reply.

"It's against the rules."

She rolls her eyes. "You and your rules."

A sigh comes through the phone. "They're not *my* rules."

More things he won't explain.

Best to cling to happy thoughts.

"You know, I still have that tulip you gave me."

She smiles at the bud vase across the room on the bureau. The water has long since dried up, but the blossom hasn't wilted. Fifty-eight years and still alive.

Talk about irony.

SEVENTEEN

Moira rubbed her temples as she slipped out of the dim gymnasium. A heavy metal wail chased her into the hall. Maybe her friends wouldn't notice if she called a cab and went home. She hadn't even wanted to come to the prom.

"Hey, Moira. You look beautiful."

She remembered his voice.

"How do you know my name?"

He disentangled from the shadows, stepping into the light. Though he was taller, black hair curling over his collar, his eyes were the same—the mesmerizing shift of blue and brown and green and gray. He stared at her, and she fidgeted, suddenly wishing the sleeves of her satin dress weren't so puffy.

"I know a lot of things." He shuffled his feet and swallowed hard. "Sorry if that sounds weird."

She flashed a shy smile.

"I'm just glad you're real. My mom said I made you up. Trauma from finding Gramps dead." Moira reached out a tentative hand and smoothed the lapels of his sports coat.

He leaned into her touch.

"Real is relative."

She started to ask what that meant, but he took her hand and guided it to his shoulder.

"Dance with me."

His arm curled around her waist, and together they moved in stiff, awkward circles. The muffled glam rock faded to something slower. He smelled of cardamom and sandalwood. His hand skimmed her back, flitted across her shoulder, stroked her hair. She relaxed and laid her head on his chest.

"I could die happy right now."

He stiffened.

"What?" Moira looked up into his eyes. The blackness she remembered when he'd touched Gramps had returned.

"It's not you." His voice sounded hollow.

A couple of girls from Moira's class staggered through the gym's doors. They reeked of pot. Giggling and wobbling on their high heels, they bumbled toward the main entrance.

The boy frowned.

"I have to go."

"You just got here." Moira grabbed at his hand. "I don't even know your name."

The black eyes flickered, for a moment speckled with robin's egg blue. He pulled a single blood-red tulip out of nowhere and tucked it behind her ear.

"I have many names."

Tires squealed outside.

Void consumed the flecks of blue.

"You can call me Ajrail."

He turned, and in two steps, disappeared out the door. Moira followed but found the parking lot deserted.

♀

"You know, I blamed myself for those girls." Moira pauses to catch her breath. It whistles in her throat.

"It wasn't your fault, my love."

"I could see they were high." She makes a helpless gesture with her hand, forgetting he can't see. "I should have stopped them."

Ajrail makes a shushing noise. "You couldn't have. It was their time."

Moira carries on, barely listening. "But I had the tulip, and the memory of our dance." A thrill goes through her. What she feels for him never gets old. "You were *real*."

He murmurs something she takes as assent.

"It wasn't until Desert Storm that I realized how it all connected."

TWENTY-FIVE

The radio crackled, but Moira didn't take her eyes off the dusty road.

"Somebody grab that. I'm driving here."

It wasn't her job to man the damn comms. The armored truck grumbled, and the wheel jerked in her hands as she maneuvered around some rubble.

Movement in her peripherals caught her eye. She turned her head and met a familiar seafoam green gaze.

"Ajrail?"

He lounged in the passenger seat, dressed in desert camo, seeming unaffected by the oppressive heat. Sorrow shadowed his face.

"Remember, darling, this isn't your fault."

"What—"

A roar and a flash of light drowned out her question before the world went dark.

When she woke, her ears felt stuffed with cotton. She recognized the makeshift lights and rough cots of the 47th Field Hospital in Bahrain. Sandalwood and spice drifted below the scents of iodine and the salty tang of the sea. She struggled to sit up.

"Easy now." Ajrail cupped her elbow but let her do the work herself.

She shook her head, trying to order her thoughts. They bounced around as if they too had been blasted by the IED. Ajrail had been in the truck. No. That couldn't be right. She looked up at him, his brown eyes morphing to hazel. It reminded her of the desert's shifting sand.

"What are you doing here?"

"There's not a lot of time to explain."

He slipped his hand down her arm and intertwined his fingers in hers. A swarm of bees hummed in her stomach.

Moira eyed the empty cots around her.

"The others?"

"Mostly bumps and bruises. They've released everyone but Murphy." He gave her hand a gentle squeeze. "Not their time."

Hazel darkened to black.

"What aren't you telling me?"

"Private Murphy."

The desert heat turned cold.

"No. The 47th is amazing. They'll fix him."

"His name is in the Book. I'm here to usher him across." He glanced at his watch. "In eleven minutes."

Moira pulled her hand from his grip and stuck her head between her knees, trying not to throw up.

"Breathe, sweetheart."

Even in her distress, the endearment made her heart flutter.

Ajrail touched her shoulder.

"Don't let him die alone."

Moira swallowed back the bile that threatened and struggled to her feet. She met Ajrail's black-eyed gaze.

"For Murphy."

He nodded and held out his hand. She didn't hesitate to take it.

♀

Moira takes a steadying breath before speaking again. She should put on the oxygen mask, but there isn't much time.

"You know, the real guilt came from the fact that I was desperate to see you, regardless of the cost. It's why I became a hospice nurse. At least I knew when you and your black eyes arrived, you brought release."

Ajrail's voice softens. "Their names—"

"Yes, yes. Their names were in the Book. Still, it was weird that my joy coincided with others' pain."

She doesn't dare add out loud that it was all worth it. She'd do it again, relive those brief moments she'd spent with him.

For a time, they say nothing. Only Moira's ragged breaths fill the silence. A vortex drags at her, and her limbs grow heavy.

Ajrail clears his throat. "So, is that why you called today, dear one? To reminisce? Or is there something else on your mind?"

She tries to laugh—he is always so intuitive—but it sets off a coughing jag. Her lungs feel filled with glass shards. The oxygen mask is out of reach and her arms are no longer under her control. Her words slur.

"I told you. I called to RSssVP for death."

He sputters, but she labors on.

"I found a way around your ssstupid Book..."

"Moira! What have you done?"

The phone slips from between her ear and shoulder. She focuses, not on the empty pill bottle on the bedside table, but the scarlet tulip. Its petals have begun to wilt.

♀

Mist swirls like windblown confetti. Moira takes a deep breath and slowly lets it out. No pain. She laughs. Though the sound escapes her lips, it goes nowhere—two-dimensional music notes that fall in a heap by her feet.

"Hello?" Like a python with a mouse, the fog swallows her cry.

She takes a step. Another. Alone in a sea of unrelenting white, it seems as if she hasn't moved. With no horizon, one direction is as good as another. She runs. Her legs strain, her heart pounds, lungs fill with air that has no flavor.

A chorus of celestial voices echo, *Moira, Moira, Moira, Moira.*

She skitters to a halt. "Ajrail?"

The mist shrinks, folding in on itself. Ajrail appears, wearing robes of clouds and stardust. A trio of ebony wings sprout from his back, each covered in countless eyes. Turquoise, like the Mediterranean. Golden lion's eyes. Browns as rich as the earth and storm-lashed grays. Topaz. Citrine. Jade. A thousand more colors she can't name. None of them are black.

He stretches his wings, and the eyes blink lazily.

Moira shivers as he turns his face toward her. Above a thin-lipped mouth and a severe nose, two inky, bottomless wells peer into her soul, blind but all-seeing.

This is unexpected. You see me as I am.

She breathes in his familiar scent—sandalwood and spice. Still her Ajrail, despite the wings.

"I don't care what you look like. We can finally be together."

She steps closer, but he holds up a hand. A tear trickles from a sandstone eye.

Mortals can't stay in the Betwixt. It exists only as a bridge, where I usher souls from the realm of the living to what comes next.

Behind him, a door creaks open, calling in siren song. People crowd the threshold. Backlit with brilliant white light, she can't quite make out their faces.

Moira glances at Ajrail and holds out her hand.

"Then come with me."

He folds his wings flat, and for a moment his image shimmers, becoming the awkward teen she'd danced with at prom.

I can't. It's against the rules.

"You and your rules." The words taste bitter on her tongue.

An invisible cord pulls her toward the Other Side. She takes a hesitant step towards the door, then stops.

"I don't know if I can. We've been together my whole life."

Ajrail shakes his head.

Those were only moments. Beautiful moments, but it wasn't living. I could never be yours. He gestures toward the crowd beyond the door. *They were the ones who were truly there for you.*

Gramps harrumphs, but his eyes twinkle in welcome. Moira's mother waves as she bounces on her toes. Murphy, his hair buzzed high and tight, winks and snaps a jaunty salute. She gives him a small smile back.

In the distance, music plays. The scents of bar-b-que and fresh cut grass waft through the door. Antique roses remind her of the grandmother she'd barely had time to know. Children shriek with laughter, and someone calls, "Kids! Slow down!" but it holds no urgency, only indulgence. What mischief can they get into here? Something deep inside her wants to find out.

The weight of a thousand eyes makes Moira turn.

"Ajrail? Why me?"

His image shifts to the round-faced boy who had taught her how to skip rocks.

It wasn't your time, and still you saw me. There's magic in you. His lips quirk into a rueful smile. *Perhaps even the Angel of Death wants to be seen.*

Moira takes two steps and leaps into his arms. Raven wings wrap themselves around her. For a fragment of eternity, she breathes him in.

Go now. Find your peace.

He gives her a gentle push towards the door. One by one, he closes his multi-hued eyes.

Only the Void watches as Moira squares her shoulders and crosses over to the Other Side.

Navigating the Dark

Thunder volleyed across the hollow and shook the house. Chipped plates rattled in the china hutch, and a cat-shaped shadow darted under the loveseat—the ghost of the smoke-gray tom she had stopped feeding years ago. She still bought the cans, lining them up in the cupboard like soldiers deployed for battle.

Here, kitty. Dinner time!

When the lights went out, they didn't flicker in advance; the darkness swallowed the dusty glow from the bulbs in a single gulp. Hands shaking, she struck a match. Its halfhearted flicker died without igniting the wick on the hurricane lantern. She tried again. The curtains fluttered as icy fingers slipped through the warped windowpane and pinched out the flame. Matchbox empty, she sighed and made her way through the blackened parlor.

The wood felt silky and cool beneath her bare feet as she shuffled along, not daring to lift her toes off the floor. She knew the route by heart, but the thought of impaling herself on spikey jacks hobbled her stride.

How many times have I told you—pick up your toys when you're done with them?

The phantom cat padded along beside her on silent paws.

A burst of incandescence brought a moment of daylight to the room. Before her, a river of wide-board pine stretched, polished by generations of footsteps. Lightning surrendered to thunder, but her feet carried on, the flash reassuring the way forward was clear.

She'd read the trick to navigating a maze was to keep one hand in contact with the wall. She reached out. Unlike the Minotaur's stone labyrinth, the wallpaper was satiny under her fingers though it peeled up at the seams to expose rough patches of horsehair plaster. She imagined the labyrinth-beast's fetid breath on her neck and sweat pebbled her lip. Jaw clenched, she stumbled forward. Her palm found the doorframe and she sidled into the hall.

You can't catch me, I'm the gingerbread man!

The dark turned framed photos on the walls into indistinct squares. She couldn't see the scenes, but her mind's eye remembered. A lacy white dress posed next to a formal suit. Swaddled infants. The boys at t-ball, graduation, posed in front of new houses with new families. There was even a snap of the late cat, asleep on an overstuffed settee. Her chest tightened, unable to contain the emotions that came with the picture book of memories.

Through an open door, storm light painted a rectangle on the carpet. For a syncopated heartbeat, a frozen sea of Kodachrome eyes stared at her. Then the light faded and stole their faces, leaving her alone again. Not even the shadow-shapes remained to keep her company.

Time for bed, boys!

Dark-blinded, she forced her leaden feet to march on.

After a few halting steps, a whiff of stale cigarette smoke and dusty tomes oriented her. Her husband's old law school primers lined the shelves on his nicotine-stained office walls. She hadn't the heart to throw the books out. A thread of spiced cologne tied the faded bouquet together. She sucked in the familiar scent, a balm to her jangled nerves.

The cat sneezed, translucent whiskers twitching.

If you must smoke in the house, dear, can you please keep your office door closed?

Her stomach curdled as the odor soured. A dead mouse in the wall? Drat that lazy cat. Swallowing down the nausea, she pushed on through the kitchen, pausing at the back stairs.

When the children were small, she'd fastened baby gates in front of what had once been servants' access. Narrow and steep, no one had bothered to add a handrail once cooks and house staff were decades out of fashion. Once again, her hand met the wall, this time to steady, not to guide. Behind her, lightning illuminated the faded linoleum. She began to climb.

One, Mississippi. Two, Mississippi. Three, Missis—

BOOM!

The climb felt steeper than it used to. She always took the stairs slowly, but when the boys had gotten older, they'd raced up and down, leaping the steps two at a time.

You'll knock your teeth out if you fall!

A second flash cast a hunched shape at the top of the stairs. Her heart squeezed as the figure loomed above her, a twisted specter. She clutched her chest, and the reaper mimicked her. She gasped, then let out a fluttery chuckle. What a ninny to be frightened by her own shadow.

BOOM!

She hesitated, trying to catch her breath. When had she gotten so old? The air felt thin—or her lungs did—and when the next flash came, black spots danced in her vision. She tripped over the ghost cat as he wound between her legs.

She struggled to find her balance, arms windmilling, as she stumbled on the last step. Dizziness surged, and she sagged against the wall. Ridged wainscoting dug into her hip. Her ears felt stuffed with dandelion fluff. She shook her head, as if she could dislodge the feeling.

Momma had a baby, and its head popped off!

The boys loved that rhyme, flicking the yellow flower-heads off the stem and giggling like mad. She'd scold them for being crass. Now, she only regretted spoiling their fun. Children's laughter should never be squandered.

She wobbled down the corridor, then through the door of the master bedroom. Like a silver pinball, she ricocheted off the furniture: three steps to the hope chest, six to the bureau, nine more to come to rest on the edge of the four-poster bed.

Thunder grumbled, an old man protesting the newfangled reality of the fading storm. The old always protested change. She echoed his discontent—a knot burned in the center of her back. A new ache on top of all her old ones. Swinging her feet up on the bed, she sighed and sank down into floral scented pillows.

Good evening, good night, With roses covered...

By habit, she reached over to her husband's side of the bed. A fist crushed her heart as her liver-spotted hands found the dip in the mattress. Fingertips tingled and turned numb.

Her eyes drifted closed and her breathing slowed. The pain faded like morning mist and she drifted.

Sleep now blissfully and sweetly, see the paradise in your dream.

The gray wraith-cat stalked through the empty house. Who'd buy the cans of tuna now?

Ten Steps to Impress a Girl

Hercules prattled on about winning some sort of sportsball match at the first Olympics. Suppressing the urge to roll her eyes, Amara played the part of Impressed Bimbo, nursing a too-sweet appletini and ooh-ing and ah-ing at the appropriate moments.

Step One: choose the right "accomplice."

Dozens of monitors showed snippets of basketball, football, and a myriad of other ball-related activities. Cheers went up and glasses clinked when favored teams scored. Amara loathed sports bars, but allowances were made when a girl needed a divine hero with more muscles than brains.

She trailed her fingers over Hercules' broad shoulders and hummed quietly. The song wove through the air like a silk ribbon. A guy at the end of the bar went slack-jawed and dropped his beer.

Ooops! My bad.

At only three-quarters siren, Amara needed to focus if she wanted to aim her power at a specific target. She hummed a few more bars, the melody transforming from bitter-sweet to haunting. The invisible ribbon twirled Hercules' head. He paused, the anecdote about slaying a lion with his bare hands forgotten. A higher-ranking immortal would be immune to her gift, but as a demigod, he was just susceptible enough for it to ignite his spark of interest into burning desire.

She probably could've done it with her boobs alone, men like him were easy, but siren-song was quicker.

He leaned close, but Amara danced out of reach.

Step Two: make him think it's his idea.

"I hear Zeus is hosting a casino night on Saturday." She pasted on a dreamy expression. "I bet the Muses will be dressed better than Zendaya at the Met Gala."

"I'm not much of a gamer, myself." Hercules flexed. "More of a feats of strength kind of guy."

Amara cooed and the siren song-ribbon tickled his cheek. "I bet you look handsome in a tux."

A puzzled look crossed the demigod's face. Like a sheepdog with an itchy ear, he tossed his head as if trying to shake a flea—or a thought—loose.

"Roulette might be fun if I had a beautiful lucky charm like you on my arm."

"You can pick me up at eight."

♀

Step Three: lay off the chocolate croissants.

Amara sucked in a breath and wrestled with the zipper of her slinky cocktail dress. The fabric shimmered as she moved, shifting from onyx to cobalt to turquoise, as mercurial as the sea. A touch of mascara, a hint of coral pink lip gloss, and she was ready to go when Hercules rolled up in a pristine Aston Martin—top down.

For fuck's sake.

She hit her curls with another spritz of mega-hold hairspray and spent the entire ride hoping her look would come off playfully wind-tousled, not rat-nest chic. Hercules monopolized the conversation, regaling her with a play-by-play of the time he took down a hydra. He karate-chopped the air, mimicking cutting off heads, not noticing Amara's less-than-enthusiastic responses. She had a soft spot for sea monsters.

The silhouette of Hotel Olympus dominated the skyline, standing over the city in graceful lines and crisp angles. Vast panes of glass glittered in the sun and waterfalls cascaded from balcony to balcony in a paradoxical fusion of divine magic and modern architecture. A minotaur security guard stood at the entrance. He seemed spring-loaded, ready to trample any interloper who dared bring trouble to the gods' night out.

Amara let Hercules help her from the car as if she couldn't navigate the curb in her heels without assistance. Men often confused superiority with chivalry.

"Careful with the Aston, boy." The demigod tossed his keys to a satyr dressed in the hotel's colors. "She's worth more than the Amazon Queen's girdle."

Amara gave the valet an apologetic look as Hercules placed a proprietary hand on her back and guided her towards the door. The minotaur guard snorted, and a hoof scraped the ground.

"Down boy. This dish is mine tonight." Hercules flashed her a cocky grin.

Step Four: don't kick him in the nuts before you get the goods.

Amara tittered and tucked her arm in the crook of his elbow.

Inside, the ballroom had been transformed into a Vegas-style casino, gods and goddesses at the gaming tables. The entire Greek pantheon had turned out in shimmering chitons and alarmingly sheer evening gowns. Hermes spun the roulette wheel sporting a classic white tunic, and Aphrodite sprawled on a chaise, wearing nothing but mist and flowers.

Hercules led the way past the divine hordes tossing dice and playing cards. Amara pretended not to notice when the goddess of mischief pulled the Zeus card from her sleeve, adding it to the Poseidon and Hades in her hand. Three kings.

Note to self: gods cheat.

It wasn't news. Best not to let it distract her from the task at hand.

Amara scanned the room. Nymphs slipped between the gamers pouring overflowing goblets of ambrosia. Coins changed hands, both at the tables and in shadowed corners. Gods would bet on anything, from dice to wars to whether or not J.Lo and Ben Affleck were getting divorced.

Step Five: choose a deserving foil.

Dionysus, god of wine and pleasure, caught Amara's gaze and raised his glass. Merlot slopped over the rim. Heavy-lidded eyes focused on her décolletage.

Creeper.

She played coy and ducked her head, only to peer through her lashes at him. Hercules frowned.

"Ambrosia, m'lord?" A dryad server held out her tray.

The demigod snatched the proffered goblet and downed the contents in a single gulp. After a second cup, he grabbed Amara around the waist and swept her onto the dance floor. Pressed hip to hip, she crooned in his ear.

"Did you see that drunk, Dionysus, leering at me?"

Hercules' face flushed crimson, ambrosia and siren song rushing through him.

"Stay here." He shucked off his dinner jacket and thrust it into her arms.

Step Six: never take orders from a man.

The crack when Hercules punched Dionysus in the face sounded like a gunshot. Ichor sprayed from the god's nose.

Whispers crescendoed through the hall. A flutter on the old god, double down on the divine hero. Markers were exchanged, wagers made. No one stepped in. Amara had been counting on it.

Hercules bounced on the balls of his feet. "Come at me, wino."

Dionysus laughed, too drunk to feel the pain. Ichor stained his teeth and dripped from his chin. Amara stared as the golden blood pooled on the Italian marble floor. Heart in her throat, she inched closer.

Hercules tackled the wine god, and the pair slammed into a craps table. Wood splintered and green felt ripped. Dice skittered across the floor, tumbling in slow motion—six, three, nine...snake eyes.

Step Seven: make your move while everyone's distracted.

Pulling a tiny glass vial from her clutch, Amara scooped up some of the ichor. With a sleight-of-hand flourish that would make an underworld daemon jealous, the bottle disappeared down the front of her dress.

Hercules stumbled to his feet and sneered down at Dionysus. "Stop ogling my girl, old man."

The elder god cradled his head in his hands. Mutters of 'upstart godlings' and 'arrogant mixed-bloods' swept through the crowd. The muttering became a low rumble.

Step Eight: always know when it's time to go.

Amara grabbed Hercules by the arm and headed for the exit. The minotaur guard, who'd remained aloof during the fight, sniffed the air, then moved to block the way.

"Contraband." He growled the single word with the force of thunder. "Blood of the gods is forbidden to mortal kind."

The hairs on the back of Amara's neck prickled as he towered over her. The vial nestled in her bra seemed to grow hot as the guard's eyes raked over her. He snorted and took a step closer.

"Oh, shove off, you overgrown cow." Hercules flipped his collar. A splash of gold stained the snowy fabric. "A souvenir from Dionysus. Couldn't hold his own against the first Olympic warrior."

"Apologies, sir."

The guard backed down, and Amara flashed him a two-finger salute.

Step Nine: try not to gloat.

"Come on, Hercules. I know a great bakery, and I have a hankering for something sweet."

♀

The demigod was easy to convince he wasn't hungry. Amara didn't even need to tickle him with her gift. Grumbling about racial slurs and teaching the old gods a lesson, he dropped her on the sidewalk, then sped off, grinding the Aston Martin's gears. Greeks were such hotheads.

A bell chimed as Amara stepped inside the bakery. The scents of cinnamon and magic hit her nose. She straightened her dress and swallowed hard.

"Be right with you!" The kitchen witch's voice had a singsong lilt to it that sent a school of minnows diving in Amara's stomach.

The witch swept into the room and set a tray of scones on the counter.

"Oh, hi! It's you. Chocolate croissants and pixie-dust throat drops." She blushed. "Sorry, I'm better with orders than names. Amara, right?"

The witch brushed flour off her apron, unaware of the adorable smudge on her nose.

"I got you a gift..." Amara fished the ichor vial out of her bra and held it out. "Sorry, it's a little sweaty."

"Is that what I think it is?" The witch squealed in delight. "One drop and I can cook anti-arthritis cookies for an entire nursing home! How'd you get it?"

Amara grinned. "Maybe we can get a cup of coffee sometime? I'll tell you the whole story."

"I'd love that." Her fingers lingered against Amara's wrist as she reached for the vial.

Step Ten: know that kindness, not machismo, impresses the girl.

No siren song required.

Never-ending Dawn

Roy pulled the covers up to his chin and huffed. "I'm not sleepy. Tell me more about the Mad Scientist of Station Seventeen, Grandma."

"The Mad Scientist, again?" I grinned and ruffled his hair. "Let's see. Did I tell you about the time she single-handedly fought off oxygen pirates with nothing more than a fleet of cleaning bots?"

Roy nodded.

"Hmmm, how about the time she tinkered with the food replicator to make all the protein supplements taste like peppermint? One step forward for mankind..."

"...in the battle against bad breath!" Roy giggled as he finished my sentence.

"Ok, ok. You've heard that one before. How about her giant mechanical rats? The time she accidentally cured VR sickness? The living protoplasma dress she wore to the Station's annual Holiday Ball?"

I pursed my lips as he dismissed each suggestion with a shake of his head.

"Well, I guess there's only one last tale to tell. The Mad Scientist's greatest invention." I paused for effect. "The creation of a biosynthetic, highly intelligent, self-aware android."

Roy's mouth rounded in an O. "Artificials are banned by the Universal Senate!"

I ignored a twinge and forced a cheery smile. "Only if you get caught. And in fact, the Mad Scientist almost did...."

♀

When the door to the morgue swished open, Ella whipped the laser scalpel behind her back. The lights blinked on and a lab tech stopped short when he saw her.

"Dr. Tyrell? What are you doing down here?"

"Just testing a theory. I thought I'd harvest the faulty nanobots from this poor fellow to see why they misfired." The lie stuck to her tongue, like the too-sweet toffee substitute they served in the canteen.

"In the dark?" The orderly narrowed his eyes and glanced at the corpse before her on the table.

"Well..." Ella swallowed. "...I sort of got lost in thought for a moment, and the motion sensor timed out."

"That must have been some thought!" He snickered at his own wit. "They really do need to lengthen the timers though." He tapped a little musical ditty on the keypad by the door, entering his personnel code. "Can I help you?"

Ella slid the body into the particalizer and slammed the door.

"Nope. I'm finished here."

She jabbed a button, and the machine began the process of breaking the corpse into its fundamental components—carbon, nitrogen, calcium. Any oxygen would be reclaimed, and the other elements would be repurposed as necessary. An excellent invention when living on a space station three weeks away from the nearest hospitable planet. She grinned. One of her best, in fact.

The tech seemed disappointed he hadn't gotten to run the machine. He watched as she made for the door, hands in her pockets. Ella tried to keep her pace natural and unhurried. Almost there. The bulkhead door whirred as it opened, and she made her escape.

"Dr. Tyrell! You forgot to log out!"

The orderly's voice chased her down the hall, but she didn't slow. She'd never signed into the restricted area. It was best no digital record remained of her visit to the morgue.

Back in her own lab, Ella sighed and punched in the lock code to secure the room. She crossed behind her 3D bioprinter and shifted the framed "Innovator of the Year 2235" award hanging on the wall. She flipped a hidden switch. Gears clicked and pistons hissed. The bullhead slid back, and she tiptoed into her secret sublab.

A small form lay on the workbench. Tow-headed with ruddy cheeks and pudgy dimpled knees, the boy looked as if he were sleeping. He was perfect, down to the last detail. Ella reached out and touched his fingers, counting one-two-three-four-five like a new mother in the maternity ward. A smile played across her lips as she looked down at her son.

She might not be able to have children, but she loved the one she made. Even if his kind was forbidden.

Her gaze lingered on his empty eye sockets. From their depths, a bit of circuitry flashed. Ella fished in her pocket and pulled out two round orbs, complete with the optic nerves still attached.

"With these, you'll finally be able to see!"

♀

"Grandma! That's gross! She stole eyeballs and stuck them in the robot boy?" Roy squirmed in horrified delight.

I laughed and shook my head. "Of course not, silly! Who do you think she was? Doctor Frankenstein?"

"Doctor who?"

"Never mind." I patted his hand, mentally counting fingers—one-two-three-four-five. "No, the Mad Scientist used the eyes as a model for her bioprinter. You see, she knew getting the eyes right was the hardest part in making an android seem like a real boy. Not the programming or the simulated emotional responses, but the eyes, for they connect a person to their soul."

Roy looked up at me, his own baby blues wide and round. "What happened next? Did she give the android a soul?"

"It's late, sweetie. I'll tell you more tomorrow."

The boy groaned. "I'm not tired."

"Well, I am." I fluffed the pillows and brushed a dirty-blond curl off his forehead.

"When can we go to Station Seventeen? It's boring here. No one lives planetside anymore."

I smothered a sigh. Little boys were too inquisitive for their own good. Just last week, he asked if we could start a height chart next to the door because he felt certain he'd start growing taller soon.

"Go to sleep now. We'll talk more in the morning."

I leaned down and kissed his soft, warm cheek. Slipping a finger behind his ear, I pressed a little lump and switched him into sleep mode. My knees creaked as I stood and shuffled to the door. Soon I'd have to wipe his memories and reboot his operating system. Again.

Outside the window, a red sun was setting, painting the sky crimson and orange. Opposite, a blue-white sun rose. Had it really been fifty years of never-ending dawns? I coughed into my elbow with a phlegmy rattle and wondered if I'd have the strength to shut down Roy for good when the time came.

A Coven is Forever

An overweight pug shot Dorothy a reproachful look from the davenport as the doorbell rang.

Are you going to get that?

Dorothy huffed and patted her steel-gray bun. That dog was definitely getting fat—spending his days on the couch cushions and doing nothing to earn his keep.

"Go! Chase mice or something."

He blinked.

Mice? Really? What am I, a cat?

"Well, at least make yourself useful. There's a goblin infestation in the pantry."

He ignored her and curled onto the pillow, settling in for a snooze. Dorothy t'sked. She'd never asked for a familiar. But here he was anyway, making himself at home and getting hair all over the sofa. Thank goodness she wasn't allergic.

The doorbell chimed again.

"I'm coming, I'm coming!"

She opened the door to find her two best friends. Right on time, as always.

Minnie wore a prim yellow cardigan and had dirt under her fingernails. She held out a bouquet of oversized gardenias. She'd probably come straight from the garden. Botanicals were her specialty, and she was constantly tinkering with some new tea blend when her grandkids came to visit. The potions and poisons she kept under lock and key, of course.

Behind her, Judy limped up the steps, leaning heavily on a wooden cane. She was a tiny, hunched woman with a halo of lilac-white curls and deep lines crossing her face as if she'd been left out in the sun for too long. An over-exaggerated grimace twisted her mouth as the cane tapped on the stone.

Dorothy took the flowers and stepped back to allow the women in. As soon as the door closed behind them, Judy straightened up, limp disappearing. Even the wrinkles on her face seemed fainter.

"Minnie. Judy." Dorothy punctuated her greetings with a welcoming smile.

Judy slung an arm over the taller woman's shoulders. "Hiyas, Dot."

Minnie giggled. "I see that anti-arthritis potion I gave you last week is working."

"It's amazing! I feel like a teenager again." Judy laid a finger against her nose and winked. "I just have to remember to keep up the limp, so the neighbors don't get suspicious."

Ladies. I'm trying to sleep here.

"Hush, dog." Dorothy flicked her fingers at him. "Come on in, girls. I set up in the dining room."

She popped the flowers into a vase, set them on the lowboy, then led the way down the hall.

In the center of the room, a table held a tea service for four. The carpet had been rolled up and tucked against the wall, exposing a large circle painted on the antique floorboards. Her late husband, may he rest in peace, would have been horrified she'd ruined the hardwood. Too bad. Witchcraft had been a far more interesting hobby to take up in retirement than knitting. And the girls had been eager to join her little coven.

Judy raised an eyebrow, taking in the black candles that had replaced the usual white tapers. As their resident demonology expert, she'd probably guessed what Dorothy had in mind, but she said nothing.

The three women settled into straight-backed chairs. The dining room was more formal than their usual spot in the cozy kitchen, but Dorothy figured today needed a little more gravitas.

Minnie reached for the teapot, but Dorothy slapped her hand away.

"Ouch! What's this all about, then, Dottie?"

Dorothy folded her hands in her lap. "The children are coming for a visit."

"That's nice, but—"

"They want to put me in Sunny Acres Retirement Home."

Her friends grumbled.

"No! That place is filled with reapers and ghouls!"

Judy leaned in, her voice in a conspiratorial whisper.

"Remember old Beth Todoro? She broke her hip, and her kids sent her there. Within a month, she was a drooling, mindless mess. They called it sudden-onset dementia, but rumor has it there's a memory vampire over there."

Minnie paled. "A memory vampire?"

"They feed on your experiences, suck them right out of your head, and before you know it, bam!" She slammed the butt of her cane on the floor. "You're wearing diapers and shuffled off to the memory ward."

Minnie patted Dorothy's hand. "We won't let that happen to you, dear. Just tell us what you're planning."

Dorothy took a deep breath and looked to Judy for support. The lilac-haired woman shrugged and made a 'get on with it' motion with her hand.

"The suggestion potions you've been making, Min, are just not strong enough. The kids have stopped listening to my 'I'm fine here on my own' suggestions."

You're not on your own.

Dorothy glanced down at the pug at her feet. How he managed to pop from one place to another without attracting attention was beyond her. Must be a familiar power.

"I'm not sure if I told them I had a magical dog, they would be reassured."

The pug huffed through his squished snout.

Their loss.

Judy rapped her knuckles on the table. "Focus. What's the plan, then?" She flashed a sly smile, as if she already knew.

Dorothy cleared her throat. "Demon spit. You're the potion wiz, Min. You know, just a drop would make the suggestion potions so much stronger."

Minnie groaned. "Oh no, Dottie, not again." She fanned her face with her hand. "We barely survived the last summoning!"

"Do you have a better idea on how to get the kids off my back? They mean well, but—"

Judy interrupted. "But they're blissfully unaware of the dangers of ghouls and memory vampires at Sunny Acres, yes we know."

"Or the terrible food they serve in those places." Dorothy wrinkled her nose with a dramatic flair, trying to lighten the mood.

Minnie sputtered, then clamped her jaws shut.

"Loosen up, Minnie-Moo." Judy jostled her with an elbow. "I've got a perfect demon in mind. A bureaucrat, not a make-a-deal-for-your-soul type."

Dorothy snickered behind her hand.

"What? Even Hell needs paper pushers. We'll just summon her up real quick. It won't be a big thing."

"That's what you said last time, and I was nearly impaled with a turkey baster." Minnie shivered.

"Nearly. *Nearly* isn't actually. Besides, it's either this, or Dot gets sent to the waiting arms of the memory vampire." She shot an apologetic look to her friend. "What's it going to be?"

Minnie swallowed hard, her cheeks pink. She nodded once, as if unable to speak.

"Thanks, ladies. I'll be forever in your debt." Dorothy clasped a hand over her heart. "So, what's first, Judy?"

"It'll be a group effort. Last time we made the mistake of not combining our powers and it made the circle too weak. Dot, is the tea ready?"

Dorothy mumbled a few words under her breath, and steam poured from the teapot. She nodded in satisfaction.

"What's the tea for?" A look of horror crossed Minnie's face as realization dawned on her. "Ew! Demon backwash."

The other two ignored her revulsion, concentrating on the ritual.

"Ok, now we'll light the candles..."

Soon, a warm glow filled the room. The dog's eyes reflected copper, a bored look on his face. Judy rummaged in her purse and pulled out a foil-wrapped breakfast bar. She passed it around and encouraged them all to take a bite. Minnie raised her eyebrows but did as she was told.

"Next step—everyone up!"

Dorothy jumped to her feet, with Minnie close behind. "Now what?"

Judy smirked. "Dance."

"Dance? We're summoning a demon with a ninety-eight-cent protein bar and a shuffling two-step?"

Oh, for crying out loud.

"Shhh!"

Judy glared at them over the top of her bifocals, as if to remind them she was the demon expert. Laughing, the other two women twirled around the circle, each dancing to a tune in their own minds. Dorothy carried out a sedate waltz, while Minnie executed an awkward jitterbug.

Raising her hands over her head, Judy took a deep breath.

"Focus your power, girls!" She dropped her arms and shouted, "Bath'taz, with your true name, I summon you!"

The candles guttered out. A mustard-yellow swirl of fog appeared within the circle. Slowly, it solidified into two legs, two arms, two curling ram horns, and a pair of leathery wings. The demon wore faded jeans and a flowered peasant blouse that didn't quite hide her muffin top. A pair of glasses perched on the top of her head and ink smudged the side of her hand as if she'd just been elbow-deep in paperwork.

She ogled the coven and rolled her eyes. "Oh, for fuck's sake. Summoned by a bunch of granny witches."

Dorothy tutted. "Language."

Bath'taz snapped her wings open, fire crackling in her eyes.

"I may work in accounting, but I'm still a card-carrying member of the Legion of Darkness. Watch yourself, girl."

"I'm eighty-two! Who are you calling girl?"

"Talk to me in seven or eight centuries, witchling." The demon reared to her full height, horns brushing the ceiling. "Now, how strong is your magic?"

Her eyes flashed black, and teacups rattled in their saucers. Minnie shrank back as the demon tested the circle of power containing her.

"Hold, ladies! We're stronger together!" Wisps escaped Dorothy's bun, writhing like gray serpents in the energy-charged air.

Tiny flakes chipped away from the painted circle as the demon battered against it. She grinned.

"I'm going to use your blood for ink and add your eyeballs to my abacus!"

Judy groaned and Dorothy poured everything she had into the magical barrier. It wasn't going to hold.

Like a soap bubble, the mystical barricade popped, and the demon roared. Overhead, the ceiling cracked, stucco dust showering down. Bath'taz lunged, and Minnie stumbled aside just in time to avoid a curved talon to the throat.

The demon spun. Her spiked tail swept across the table. The tea set fell to the floor and shattered.

Judy slashed with her cane, but one huge wing slapped into her. She landed on her backside with an audible oof!

Bath'taz grabbed a chair and hurled it across the room. Dorothy ducked. The demon snatched up a second chair.

Need a little help?

The coven shouted in unison:

"Yes!"

"Yes!"

"Please!"

More gracefully than one would expect for his size, the pug leaped over the shattered pottery and padded over to the demon. He danced around her cloven feet, jumping up on her legs.

"Aaaaa-choooooo!"

Dorothy recoiled as snot splattered her cheek.

The demon froze, holding the dining room chair over her head.

"Dogs! I hate dogs. I'm allergic." She seemed to stifle another sneeze. "Get it away from me!"

Judy held up a finger as she wheezed and coughed. It took her a moment to catch her breath and struggle to her feet.

"We'll wrangle the dog, but you need to do something for us."

Bath'taz sniffled and wiped her nose on the back of her hand. Her eyes looked red and puffy.

"Anything. Strike the deal so I can go back to hell!"

Dorothy rubbed a bit of plaster off her nose.

"Just a smidge of saliva was all we needed." She glanced forlornly at the broken teacups. They'd been her favorites. "We could have had tea, like civilized...people. But now I don't know how we'll collect it." Her voice rose in a wail.

Minnie rummaged in her pocket and pulled out a glass vial. Four pairs of eyes stared at her—two human in brown and blue, a set of bloodshot demon eyes, and the deep puppy-dog's of the pug.

"What? A girl never knows when she might want to mix a wee potion!"

The demon cackled. "I like you, grannies. Very sassy." She loomed over Minnie, who, to her credit, only trembled a little when the vial was plucked from her hand.

Bath'taz unstoppered the cork and hawked a fat, green loogie.

"Um...thank you?"

Dorothy leaned down and picked up the pug.

Hey! Watch the tail.

She hugged him to her chest. Perhaps having a familiar wasn't that bad, after all.

With a final sneeze, the demon poofed away, leaving behind a strange bouquet of brimstone and granola in the air.

The coven stared at each other. Blood oozed through a rip in Minnie's jeans. A purple lump was rising over Dorothy's eye. Judy was limping for real this time. At least she hadn't broken her hip.

Dorothy sighed, dejected. "I think we're going to need to use the demon snot to super-charge a healing potion."

Judy flashed her friend a reassuring grin. "Don't worry, Dot. We'll figure out another way to convince your kids not to send you to Sunny Acres."

Minnie slipped her arm through Dorothy's. "Of course we will. We survived a demon. We can survive a pair of pushy kids, too!"

They're right, you know. And you're not alone here. Girlfriends and covens stick together.

Dorothy smiled. "Leave the mess, for now, girls. Let's go to the kitchen. I could use a drink."

Judy snickered. "As long as you're not serving tea."

Top of the Charts

"And She Was" Talking Heads, 1985

Jenn leaned against the bar and watched a girl in a miniskirt and huge earrings circle the dance floor. The gold hoops swayed in rhythm with her hips, but her teased bangs remained Aqua Net stiff.

Jenn's heart frog-flopped.

"Hey! Little Miss Broody!"

Jenn dragged her gaze from the girl. The bartender's Freddie Mercury mustache quirked over a grin as he slid a neon green monstrosity toward her. It came with a plastic cocktail sword impaling a cherry.

"Courtesy of Preppy Boy." Mustache pointed to the end of the bar, rolling his eyes.

Preppy had the collar popped on his salmon-colored polo. Jenn stole a glance at Dancing Girl, then studied the drink, wondering if the requisite stilted conversation with a dude she'd never screw was worth the free booze. She toyed with the sword.

"You could just tell him, you know."

Jenn frowned. "Tell him?"

What does Mustache think he knows?

"Whatever, girl." He swapped the saccharine cocktail for a beer and winked.

"Silent Running" Mike + The Mechanics, 1986

Despite a sugar-dusting of snow, Jenn didn't feel the cold, just a numbness running from her toes to the void inside her ribcage.

A rumble caught her attention. She turned around, walking backward, and stuck out her thumb. Headlights spotlighted her.

Mustache leaned across the passenger seat and flicked open the door.

"Get in the car, bitch. You'll freeze your tits off."

Jenn clambered in and held her hands to the heater.

"Where to, Miss Broody?"

"Anywhere but here," Jenn said.

Away from Dancing Girl and her laughter.

"I'm sorry. I know it took ages for you to muster up the courage to say something to her."

Of course, he'd seen the whole thing.

Mustache squeezed her knee. "You can do better than that diva, any day of the week."

"Brilliant Disguise" Bruce Springsteen, 1987

"One beard, reporting for duty!" Mustache gave Jenn a jaunty salute.

She bit back a nervous giggle. "Try to behave, will you?"

"No worries. Moms love me."

Even homophobic ones?

She kept the thought to herself. He knew the deal; took his earrings out for the ruse and everything.

"Thanks for playing boyfriend. Family weddings suck."

Mustache offered his arm, like some mockery of Prince Charming. "If the best man's hot, I'm gonna need his number."

"I'll Be There for You" Bon Jovi, 1989

The scent of industrial bleach filled Jenn's nose. It was easy to find his room—the only one with no one bustling in and out. Not even nurses. There wasn't a scarlet letter on the door screaming *AIDS!* but there might as well have been.

He looked too small in the hospital bed, all stick arms and legs.

Still has that stupid mustache.

She choked on a laugh. Or a sob. It could've been either.

He shrank back when she reached for him.

"Don't be a douchebag." She forced a smile to show she was only teasing.

Wrapping her fingers around his, Jenn spent a silent eternity holding his hand when no one else would.

"I Remember You" Skid Row, 1990

The circle of mourners got smaller at each funeral, but Jenn kept going. Someone had to.

How long before I'm all that's left?

So Someone Remembers

Colm kicked his chair and huffed. "This is stupid." He jabbed a finger at the blue-green drawing in the book. "There's no such thing as an *ocean*." He stumbled over the unfamiliar word.

"There used to be, before ***It*** swallowed them up." A shiver tiptoed down Teranika's spine with spidery footsteps. She rushed on, better to talk about long gone seas than ***It***.

"Ah, I wish you could have seen the ocean. Silvery and vast, briny water filled with fish and all manners of mystical creatures."

She concentrated, wriggling her fingers in a complicated sequence under the table. The waves in the picture surged. A head with seaweed green tresses emerged from the water. Bright eyes seemed to look out of the page. A phantom salt breeze caressed Teranika's cheek, pressing damp kisses against her brow.

"The mermaids used to come to shore on the nights of the full moon."

A painted ribbon of silver light guided the finned woman to shore.

"When they touched the sand, their tails would split into legs, and they'd transform into women. If you listened closely, you could hear them sing as they combed each other's hair."

"Mom, seriously. That's just silly. Moons and fish and mermaids and monsters are just stories." He rolled his eyes. "Why do I have to read about all this stuff?"

Teranika sighed and let the illusion go. The waves stilled, flat ink on the page. "So someone remembers."

Birdlike, Colm cocked his head. Tufts of hair, the same dusky red as a robin's breast, stuck out around his ears. Teranika didn't need to dip into his thoughts to taste his confusion. It smelled of wood smoke and anise and ground hugging fog. More things that no longer existed.

The boy looked at her with pleading puppy eyes and she shook her head.

"Fine, go outside and play. But st—"

"I know, I know! Stay away from the edge." Without putting the books away, Colm slipped out of his chair and darted out into the yard as if afraid she'd change her mind.

Teranika clucked her tongue and tidied up after her son. From time to time, she peered through the open door to check on him. His shoes were untied, the laces dangling as he climbed their lone fruit tree. He plucked thumbnail-sized maroon orbs, stuffing them in his mouth and letting the sweet juice dribble down his chin.

She watched him, wishing she could remember the fruit's name.

Chew. Swallow. Spit out the tiny stones that lived in the heart of the firm flesh.

He aimed for the edge, the nothingness beyond their little oasis. Most of the pits landed along the line where the grass thinned to feathery wisps and the ground crumbled away. The pits that breached the verge were destined to fall for eternity.

Teranika steeled herself. For the moment, the boy was occupied. Time to measure. She needed to know if their floating island was being nibbled away by the emptiness.

She opened a cupboard and pulled out a ball of yarn, then tucked a pair of sewing scissors into her apron pocket. Perhaps she wouldn't need them. Maybe ***It*** wasn't chewing on their sanctuary, for she'd been feeding ***It*** other things, intangible things. Like the word for the sweet stone fruit that grew on the tree. Names had such power.

She gave ***It*** memories, too. How the waves had sounded as they battered the shore, back before ***It*** drank the sea. Had the surf thundered against barnacle-covered rocks, or rushed along the sand like the rustle of silk? ***It*** had devoured each remembered moment with insatiable relish. And when ***It*** was done feeding, only the nothingness remained.

Clutching the yarn, Teranika headed outside. She sidled up to the edge but fixed her gaze on the ground. She could feel the lure of the void. ***It*** hovered in the darkness, waiting to gobble her up. The inky vacuum swirled and danced. There was movement in the velvet nothingness, hypnotic and predatory. She couldn't see the malevolent presence, but she felt ***Its*** never-ending hunger.

Teranika set her shoulders and weighed down the end of the yarn with a rock. Taking slow, even steps, she paced around the miniature island, unraveling the ball. The twisted lamb's wool, dyed pale yellow with chamomile blossoms, slipped through her fingers as she walked.

Past the straggly garden filled with purple, moth-eaten cabbages and limp-topped parsnips. She'd never been good with vegetables. Magical herbs were more her domain, poultices and poisons and potions. No need for them here, so she fed them to ***It*** ages ago—their names lost to the nowhere.

She snorted. Maybe she should have fed ***It*** the cabbages or the moths, but no, ***It*** desired things more flavorful. The feel of starlight on the skin, the way wood nymphs had danced in sun-dappled forests, the tender memories of young love. Not stinky, bitter vegetables that no one wanted to eat or boring, powdery-winged insects.

Teranika inched around the well, playing out another measure of yarn, both rough and soft against her fingertips. The fieldstone ring perched on the edge of their refuge, teetering on the precipice between solid and ephemeral. For years she had lowered the bucket, cranking uncounted lengths of rope into the well's depths before hearing an echo of a splash. The reservoir was deeper than the island. She tried not to think about how that could possibly be.

And yet in the deep of night, it always came back to haunt her. She imagined the island as a rocky disc floating in a sea of emptiness. The cozy cottage sat alone on the slab, a final relic of a world swallowed by the void. Lanterns shone from the windows, their golden squares the only light in the darkness. She had long since fed the stars and moon to the creature.

In the yard, the fruit tree grew strong. She pictured its roots snaking through soil and stone to dangle below. Blind, wriggling worms that burrowed deep, only to find there was naught on the other side. The nothingness was unending.

Teranika shook off the image and kept pacing. Past the tangle of brambles behind the small cottage. Fragrant pink flowers bloomed in a thicket by the back door. The silken petals meant something, but she had allowed ***It*** to dine on the memory many cycles ago. Still, there was an echo of feeling, deep in her core. Not the paradoxical soft and fierce sentiment that she harbored for her son, but something older that had once burned with the intensity of the sun.

In the depths of the void, ***It*** howled, annoyed that she clung to the echo.

A few more steps and she passed the headstone. She trailed her fingers on the pitted marble. The name was long gone, licked away by ***Its*** questing tongue, but she remembered a bushy red beard and twinkling eyes. She once laid on his broad chest, skin against skin. His laughter had rumbled through her. Whoever he had been, she hoarded these lingering images, tucking them deep away lest ***It*** scented them. Her face flushed, and she clenched her fists. ***It*** would not have these fractured moments.

She didn't know why it was important. Only that it was.

Back to where she started, Teranika played out the end of the yarn ball. She still had an arm's length in her hands. A sharp-clawed fear worried at the inside of her stomach.

She glanced up. In the yard, Colm giggled as he flipped upside down, hanging from the branch of the stone fruit tree. A fat robin perched in the upper branches, supervising the boy's revelry.

Teranika angled her body to block the boy's view. She felt in her pocket for the scissors, clipped the damning length of excess yarn. Best he didn't know their sanctuary was shrinking.

She tossed the bit of string over the edge.

The something in the nothing swelled.

It hovered in the void, waiting to swallow the tidbit down. A smudge of soot-gray writhed in the darkness, neither flesh nor smoke. ***It*** had no shape.

It shifted.

A lizardlike creature with leathery wings and teeth as long as sabers.

A robed figure, hood pulled low to hide its face.

A church grim. A banshee. A wraith.

No matter the form, two black-ember eyes burned with a gnawing hunger. The shadows of all that ***It*** had eaten swirled in their depths.

She scowled and stamped her foot. "I've given you so much. And yet you still chew on the island. It is the last vestige of Earth."

So hungry.

Teranika glared into the nothingness.

Not enough. Never enough.

"I gave you the mountains and the valleys."

Thirsty.

Teranika rolled the yarn into a tight ball—a little smaller than it had been this morning.

"You sipped the rivers, swallowed down the lochs, guzzled the oceans. You drank the rain and let the snows melt on your tongue."

More.

"I will give you the robin. The memory of its cheery song. Another fair name to devour."

Not enough. So very hungry.

The void cast a covetous look at the island, the small cottage, the laden fruit tree. ***It*** plucked at the grass. A shower of soil streamed into ***Its*** maw.

"No. We need this bit of rock and dirt to survive."

Then give me something more. The boy's name.

It flexed and grinned. A blade of green grass stuck in ***Its*** teeth.

Perhaps I'll finally be sated.

♀

The woman blinked.

By the base of a tree, a ginger-haired boy fiddled with his grubby shoelaces. He stumbled and something deep inside her screamed. She lunged for him, snagging his shirt and yanking him back from the edge. Her heart thundered in her chest in a silent, syncopated rhythm.

The void pulsed. ***It*** smelled of hot coals and copper coins and singed hair. Angry.

She wanted to howl—*you can't have him.* The need to keep him safe from the ravenous creature overwhelmed her. She wasn't sure why, only that it was the only thing that mattered.

The child smiled up at her, his lips stained crimson with fruit juice. He had the sweetest dimples and a cowlick at the back of his head. She smothered an urge to smooth it down. He reminded her of someone. She'd remember in a moment. Surely she would.

She breathed in the scent of wood smoke and ground hugging fog that wafted in the air. Colm.

"Hey, Mom! Can we look at the books again? I want to read more about the mermaids."

Mom? The woman's stomach roiled. She had no memory of being a mother. She was...who was she? Did it matter?

"Mermaids?"

Colm's dark eyes held wisdom beyond his age. "I think you're right. Someone needs to remember."

There's No Such Thing as 'Til Death Do Us Part

Agnes frowned at the knock on the front door and shook wood shavings off her faded housecoat. It was uncivil to drop by someone's home without warning. For a moment, she considered playing deaf—at her age folks would excuse small moments of rudeness as infirmity and she wasn't above capitalizing on their biases. The knocking came again, more insistent. She sighed, set the chisel on her repurposed sewing table, and closed the door to her craft room before heading to the foyer.

At the front window, she twitched the curtain aside and peered out onto the porch. A tall blurry form stood, arm raised to knock again. Agnes grumbled and slid her reading glasses off her nose to hang around her neck on a rhinestone-studded chain. She'd ordered it off the Internet—with her grandson's help—the day after she found her glasses in the freezer next to the Sunday roast. Around the neck was an easier place to keep track of than the freezer, or wherever else she'd end up leaving them.

Agnes shook her head and chastised herself. Focus. Outside, the shape clarified into a handsome, broad-shouldered young man, with a strong jaw and close-cropped brown hair. He wore a carefully pressed and well-tailored navy-blue uniform. She did appreciate it when young people took care with their appearances. She clucked her tongue. And here she was in her housecoat. Well, his fault for calling unannounced.

Before he could knock again, Agnes opened the door.

"Good afternoon, officer." She cringed at the thready sound of her voice. It had once been a clear, commanding contralto.

"Ma'am. Are you..." He glanced down at a small notebook in his hand. "...Mrs. Russo? Agnes Russo?"

She nodded and perched her glasses back on her nose to read his name badge. Officer Steward. There was something familiar about his black eyes. It reminded her of the garnet ring Nicoli had given her on their twentieth wedding anniversary. Not the crimson stone itself—she wasn't daft. The boy had the same dark eyes as the jeweler. She remembered from when she'd gone in to get the ring sized. She'd wanted to exchange the gem, she favored emeralds, but Nicoli had insisted that the garnet was more appropriate. In reality, it had simply been cheaper. She circled back around—she knew this uniformed youngster.

"Billy Steward? Is that you?" She smiled and dropped her glasses to dangle from the chain. "I know your father. What a lovely man. Is he well?"

The officer shifted his feet and cleared his throat.

"Dad passed a few years back."

Agnes frowned. How had she not known that? She laid a comforting hand on the boy's arm. Despite her liver-spotted skin, she was grateful she wasn't twisted with arthritis like several of the women in her Bridge group. It took them ages to deal the cards.

"I'm so sorry. Please come in. I'll make tea." She hustled the officer into the parlor, ignoring his polite protests.

After settling him on the good settee, the one with the extra plush cushions she reserved for guests, she headed into the kitchen to put the kettle on. She fussed with the tins of fragrant dried leaves, settling on a strong, dark English tea. Good for the nerves. A flutter tickled her stomach. Exactly why was Billy here? As pleasant as it might be to have a vibrant youngster in her sitting room, she doubted he was calling socially on an old lady.

She rummaged in the lowboy and pulled out the fancy china. Nicoli wouldn't have approved—the fancy china was for her in-laws and the local minister, not a common civil servant. She smirked and pulled out the holiday silver as well. Her only regret was that she couldn't watch Nicoli squirm. The old goat. Agnes balanced the teapot, cups, and accouterments on a tray and headed back to the parlor.

"I wasn't sure if you took lemon, or cream and sugar, so I brought both."

Billy glanced at the tray.

"I'm really more of a coffee drinker."

"Cream and sugar, then."

Agnes poured, then passed the officer a teacup. She wrapped her hands around her own cup, letting the warmth seep through the delicate porcelain and into her fingers. Eyes closed, she indulged in the feeling for a half a dozen heartbeats.

When she opened her eyes, she looked up at Billy's face and raised her eyebrows. He held his teacup, frozen a few inches below his mouth, his lips curled in distaste. Kids these days with their preferences for obnoxious coffee orders. Even the thought of a Triple Verdi, No-Fat, Half-Calf, Caramel Macchi-something-or-other made her head spin. She paused when she noticed he was staring across the room.

Agnes followed his gaze. When she realized what he was looking at, she grinned. Setting down her tea, she walked over to the table, dropping her hand to caress soft black fur.

"Macintosh was my first."

Billy started. "Pardon?"

"I said, Macintosh was my first."

She enunciated the words with precision, wondering if the poor boy was a tad hard of hearing. How had he become an officer of the law? Surely, they had to pass some sort of physical. She glanced back down at the stuffed cat.

"My darling kitty accidentally got into a package of rat poison. Such a tragedy." She teased a pair of tufted ears. "I've always been a crafty person and I couldn't bear the thought of burying my sweet boy in the dank earth."

With a grimace, she trailed a finger over the cat's mangled, silent snarl.

"I didn't realize how difficult the tanning process would be. Preserving the skin was more of a challenge than I'd expected."

Billy swallowed, his Adam's apple bobbling.

"You home taxidermied your cat?"

Agnes narrowed her eyes. Had that been disapproval in his tone, the little jackanape? Years of Nicoli's censure had honed her ability to read vocal nuance.

"It's not against the law, you know. I submitted my application and paid the licensing fee." She folded her arms over her chest and sniffed. "It's important to have something to keep you busy in your 'golden years.' They say a good hobby keeps you young."

The officer paled and tugged at his collar. Wide eyes darted around the room, as if desperate to land anywhere but the stuffed cat. They lit on a blue metal tin.

"Butter cookies. My gran has the same one. It's full of buttons." He barked out an awkward, seal-like laugh.

Agnes reached for the tin and gave it a vigorous shake. It rattled.

Billy sighed, tense shoulders relaxing.

"You collect buttons too?" He took a sip of his tea.

With a chuckle, Agnes pried the lid off the tin and showed him the contents. A rainbow of glass eyeballs stared back at him. Green slitted cats' eyes. The wide, round pupils of night birds. Brown eyes the size of marbles and tiny black dots for mice and squirrels. Billy spluttered, tea dribbling down his chin.

"It's nothing, dearie. Think of it as a fur coat stretched over a wooden form." Agnes patted the stuffed cat on the head. "I've started carving my own forms now, instead of buying them online. It gives me more control."

She pointed toward the mantel. Balanced above the cold fireplace, a brown and white feathered barn owl spread broad wings. One wickedly curved talon stretched toward a tiny gray shape—a mouse poised in eternal flight. It seemed as if time had stopped for the two creatures and might resume at any moment. The owl would emit a shrill hunting cry. The mouse would squeak in fright and dive behind the carriage clock on the mantelpiece.

"The owl was roadkill, but it took me a few tries to catch its little gray friend."

Billy stammered something unintelligible.

"It was better than having a mouse in the pantry." Agnes smiled wide, showing all her teeth. "I did my friend Betty's Shar Pei a few weeks ago. Talk about a challenge. All those wrinkles! But it turned out a delight. I wish I had a photo to show you, but I haven't gotten the film developed yet."

Billy wrinkled his forehead.

"Film?"

Agnes felt the heat rise in her cheeks.

"Well, supposedly the newfangled cell phone my kids insisted I get has a camera built in, but I like being able to hold the photos in my hand, you know?"

She sat back down and smoothed her housecoat over her knees and forced her voice bright and cheery.

"But please forgive me, Billy, for being so rude. I'm sure you didn't come here to listen to an old lady prattle on about her hobbies."

The officer cleared his throat.

"Yes. I'm actually here for a wellness check." He thumbed through his notebook. "A neighbor reported that your husband Nick—"

Agnes interrupted, "Nicoli." Her nostrils flared at the conditioned response. Her husband had not believed in nicknames.

Billy nodded and jotted a note.

"Your neighbor said that she hadn't seen Nicoli in some time. She also mentioned you had stopped coming to the weekly Bridge group."

The flush on Agnes's cheeks deepened to anger. It had to be that meddlesome Rita Perkins with her bad home perm and nicotine-stained teeth. How dare she stick her nose in where it wasn't wanted? And just when things were shaping up around here. Busybodies were the epitome of rudeness.

Agnes forced herself to unclench her fists and took a deep breath.

"How kind of her to be concerned." Her voice sounded brittle in her own ears. "But Nicoli is just fine, Officer. He's away on an extended fishing trip outside of Milwaukee."

The boy had the grace to look embarrassed as he shifted in his seat.

"Is that his Buick parked out front?"

Surreptitiously wiping sweaty palms on her housecoat, Agnes thought quickly.

"It is. Nicoli doesn't like to drive long distances anymore, so he took the bus." She leaned in and offered a conspiratorial wink. "And with him out of my hair, I have more time for my little hobby, so I've been skipping Bridge. I've got a ferret in the freezer I'm just *dying* to get my hands on."

Face green, Officer Steward shot to his feet.

"Thank you so much for your time, ma'am. Everything seems in order here. I'll see myself out." He tripped over the words, as well as his own feet, in a rush to escape.

Agnes waited for the door to click shut before gathering the tea things back onto the tray and taking them to the kitchen. She resisted the temptation to run to the craft room. Instead, she carefully washed the china and patted her hands dry on the embroidered "World's Best Grandma" tea towel. She returned the cream to the fridge. A container of leftover Pad Thai caught her eye. She'd have it for dinner later. Nicoli had never let her order takeout.

A woman's rightful place is in the kitchen, preparing home-cooked meals for her family.

She'd spent a lifetime adhering to Nicoli's vision of what a woman's rightful place was. She hissed, cat-like, through her teeth. She'd had quite enough of that.

Once the kitchen was ordered, she headed back to the parlor and rummaged around in the tin of glass eyes. She clucked her tongue. None of them were quite right. Brown dog's eyes seemed too sweet. Hawk eyes, too shrewd. The liquid cow eyes seemed so gentle. Definitely not. She finally settled on a pair of beady pig's eyes that almost seemed human. She tucked them in her pocket and headed to the craft room.

"Hello, Nicoli, my dear."

Olive skin stretched over the tanning rack, topped with a thatch of thick, silver hair. He had loved to run his fingers through it, taunting his balding friends. It had been so very easy to add peanut oil to his pomade and even easier for him to unwittingly transfer the oil to his lips. She had sat, hands folded primly in her lap, as her husband's throat closed, and his eyes bulged.

Agnes balanced her glasses on the bridge of her nose and prodded his leathery cheek.

"I'm so glad the tanning didn't damage your skin. That would have been such a shame. You have such a lovely complexion."

She fished the glass pig eyes out of her pocket and laid them on the sewing table, then turned to pick up a piece of sandpaper. She hummed to herself as she smoothed the carved wooden form—sexless like a giant Ken doll.

If there were no more interruptions, she'd be able to finish up before dinner. Her chest swelled with pride. The Shar Pei had been a challenge, but this would be her greatest triumph.

"Oh Nicoli, I do love the strong and silent type." She giggled. "So much for *'til death do us part*."

Knock, Knock

When the knock came, Penny had thought it would be insistent and bold. The way she remembered him. Instead, it fluttered, hesitant, against the door like the wings of a broken bird. She might have missed it if she hadn't been waiting for it. He'd been smart to send a runner ahead to let her know he was coming.

Staring at the top of the stairs, Penny forced herself to take a step down, and a wave of memory consumed her.

The wind teased her braids as she swung back and forth. A large, warm palm splayed against her back—catching her, pushing her higher. He was her safety net and the one who challenged her boundaries.

She giggled and pumped her feet. "Higher, higher!" If he pushed just a little harder, if she perhaps pointed her toes and reached, she'd swing high enough to touch the sky.

After too many years of ashfall and sulfurous smog, she had almost forgotten what blue skies looked like. She wrenched her foot forward, lowering it to the next riser.

The thunder of feet sounded on the dock as Penny and her friends raced to be the first into the lake. She squealed and leapt. A weightless silence filled her ears as the water closed over her head, icy cold in contrast to the hot summer day. She surfaced, spluttering.

Back on the lawn, the crowd of parents laughed and cheered. His deep guffaw rumbled louder than them all. She raised a dripping hand to wave to him. When he flashed her the special smile he reserved just for her, a comfortable warmth blossomed in her chest. The crisp water no longer felt as cold.

Penny swallowed the lump in her throat. No one swam in the lakes anymore. The water burned the skin like acid. She took another step.

Outside the window, the setting sun painted the yard with streaks of gold. Penny straightened her miniskirt. He wouldn't approve, but if she distracted him, he might not notice what she had on before she slipped out for her date.

A squadron of butterflies dive-bombed in her stomach as she rubbed lipstick off her teeth. She'd stolen the tube from her mother's things. The everyday clutter he couldn't bear to give away now that it was just the two of them.

"Penny! That lowlife boyfriend of yours is here!" He couldn't keep the hint of laughter out of his faux, stern voice.

After one last glance at the mirror, she skipped down the stairs and gave him a quick peck. Whiskers tickled her lips. "I promise I'll be home by midnight. Don't wait up!"

She ignored the wistful look in his eyes as he rubbed the coral smudge off his cheek.

The knock came louder and drowned out the phantom voices. She glanced at her watch. Fifteen minutes to curfew. If she didn't let him in, the patrols would pick him up.

She forced her feet onward.

He looked odd, clean-shaven, and sporting a crisp uniform with his rucksack slung over his shoulder. She should have been proud that he was doing his part. Instead, she felt hollow. When she met his eyes, he opened his mouth, then clenched his jaw. Everything had already been said–more than once. A muscle twitched by the corner of his eye.

He reached for her, but Penny folded her arms over her chest and shrank back, unwilling to forgive him for leaving. He blinked a few times, eyes shining, then straightened his shoulders and snapped to attention, giving her a rigid salute.

When the door closed behind him, Penny crumpled to the floor. She stayed there for hours, bawling with her cheek pressed against the cold, black-and-white tiles. How could he leave her alone?

Penny choked back a sob and stumbled off the last step. Why come back now? She'd stopped hoping ages ago. His silhouette wavered through the mottled glass. They both stood motionless, separated by a door and the weight of too many years.

Time stretched like taffy. The real saltwater kind they used to buy at the summer fair. Not the post-war, synthesized crap that tasted like old rubber bands.

His shadow stepped back. She'd hesitated too long, and he was leaving.

"No!" Penny held her breath and, without taking any precautions, threw back the deadbolt and whipped open the door.

The poisoned air stung her eyes. Blindly, she grabbed his sleeve and yanked him inside, then slammed the door shut. She coughed and rubbed her burning skin. When her eyes cleared, she glanced at the figure in front of her.

He stripped off his gas mask. She only saw a stranger in a ragged uniform. A long scar ran down his cheek, and his eyes seemed dull and weary. He held his left arm stiffly, a monstrosity of plate metal, gears, and pistons, as if uncertain where flesh ended and technology began.

He smiled, and it all flooded back. In a heartbeat, he reverted to the person he'd been, the one she remembered. All the things she'd saved in her head to say to him—*Where have you been? Why didn't you write? I thought you were dead*—could wait. The years dropped away, the distance forgiven.

Penny launched into his arms and mumbled into his chest, "Welcome home, Daddy."

Recipe for Being Single in Your 40s

Five Stars

112 made it / 28 reviews / 31 photos

Recipe by: singleandlovingit47

I wish I could say this recipe was handed down to me by my mother. Or my grandmother, or my godmother. Aunts, sisters, grade schoolteachers, guidance counselors, hell, that eccentric old lady I met on the bus that one time who talked about knitting and cats the entire trip from Pittsburgh to Orlando. Instead, I had to figure it out on my own, trial-and-error style. And let me tell you, some of the errors were disastrous.

Someone should have given me this, printed out on a neat little card so I could laminate it and reference it as needed. They didn't. But I'm handing it down to you. All I ask is that you don't keep it to yourself.

Ingredients:

3.141 pounds of fortitude
2 generous gallons of self-worth*
3 bushels of independence
8 ounces of comfortable solitude
7 cups of courage**
1 thick skin, color of your choice***
2 dashes of sarcasm
A pinch of clever comebacks
Sass and style to taste

*Self-worth can be replaced with one brave facade, administered whole. Caveat: while this kind of stoic veneer is effective for beginners, it is not generally recommended for best results.

**Do not substitute. Courage is required for defying expected social standards. Without it, you will not achieve the desired results. The good news is you likely already have plenty in your cupboard, even if you don't think you do. Check behind the imposter syndrome.

***Stretched, scarred and/or misshapen skins are encouraged for use. Please do not disregard because of perceived imperfections.

Directions:

In a large mixing bowl, combine a foundation of fortitude, courage, and self-worth. Stir until the mixture forms strong peaks. Note: when using a brave facade in place of self-worth, do not over beat. Facades are brittle and tend to crumble when least expected.

In a separate bowl, sift together independence and comfortable solitude. Do not skip sifting or the confection will have lumpy moments of self-doubt and scattered instances of loneliness that will be chalky and unpalatable. Gently fold the mixture in with the foundation ingredients.

Once the concoction comes together in a cohesive psyche, scoop into the skin. Size, shape, and color of the skin are immaterial. However, texture matters—your final product will be subject to the weight of judgment and prejudice. The thicker the skin, the safer the internal identity will be.

Let the character rest. The length of time is subjective, but a little self-directed kindness, patience, and compassion go a long way here.

After resting, sprinkle with sarcasm and clever comebacks. This allows the final dish to navigate the inevitable "why are you still single" question. Responses such as *not everyone can handle this fabulousness* and *I really don't have the time, with implementing my plan for world domination and all* will do nicely. One liners, zingers, and smart aleck quips give this recipe its unique flavor and tend to shut down individuals who prefer to judge before tasting.

Optional: for the more adventurous culinary artist, sometimes brutally honest can trump sarcasm. However, do not attempt without a heaping measure of scathing poise. *I don't need a partner to prove my worth.*

Finally, add sass and style, sampling often, and cure for at least 40 years.

Best served with a complex Cabernet and accompanied by the unwavering adoration of a Labrador Retriever.

Serving size: one.

Sanctuary

Windows at night are like portals to another world. You never know what might press its face up against the glass and stare back at you.

Outside, the darkness is textured—layers of penumbra that have swallowed the landscape. I try to picture it in my mind, the sweeping lawns, the manicured gardens, but the inky silhouettes are all in the wrong places. Too big to be the pink-blossomed hollyhock spikes. Too small and twisted to be the wrought iron gate. It's as if when the light faded, the world beyond the window casing rearranged itself, morphing into something new.

There's movement, but it's indistinct, shadow on shadow. I tell myself it's a trick of imagination, wind dipping a branch on a tree I'm certain was further away from the bay window last I looked. I do not throw open the sash—not yet. In my heart, I know the night is breathless and the oak boughs are still.

Yet *something* moves. It feels familiar.

The river of white stones that make up the drive has come alive, a hooded snake nosing across the grounds. Its tongue tastes the air as it hunts for midnight prey. I sense, rather than see, for we are connected; two halves of a whole. Freed of our separate prisons for a single night.

No moonlight glitters off the stone viper's snowy scales. No star song chimes in a velvet sky. The uncanny night creature that slithers through the gardens lives in darkness with no need for such pinpricks of light to show the way.

Inside, strange newfangled electric bulbs illuminate the room at my back. I stand with reckless abandon in the window and wonder if from the gardens I make a stately portrait framed in a square of light. The night serpent shifts, fixing me with the weight of its unseen eyes. Just as I can feel it, it too knows I'm here.

Come to me.

A longing to slip into the darkness tugs at me. To run barefoot alongside the beast, feel the cool earth beneath my feet. My fingers itch to trail along its hide and trace the smooth interlocking plates. The urge to meld, forgoing limbs in favor of crushing coils, overwhelms me. It's been so long since the two of us have joined as one.

I take an impulsive step towards the window and the glass reflects my own face back at me—a translucent ghost with fathomless eyes and wispy curls escaping a dark braid. My gauzy sari leaves my arms bare. A blue-black pattern mars smooth skin. Four fingers and a thumb. I press the bruise, and its sting reminds me why I'm here.

The colossal viper shrieks, a tempest that rattles the shutters and rips clay tiles from the roof. Its long tail slams against the building, heavier than a boulder. The door shudders but holds. My face flushes and my hands clench into fists. I want to strike hard and fast. Tear down the walls that keep us apart. It's not my anger, though it feels as if it is.

I pry my fingers open, stretching them to create the mudra for Peace and Tranquility. My breath comes slow and even as I try to soothe our rage. I shake my head. The serpent's rage. Its anger is not directed at me, but at the betrayal of our separation.

For a time, I send wave after wave of calming energy to my other half. I remind it of the fear and danger that drove me here in search of sanctuary.

Father tightened his grip on my arm, crowding me against the wall. I hissed. His eyes flashed yellow as his trickster hyena magic cut me off from connecting to my serpent.

"Do you think you can disobey me, child?"

He shook me, and my head bounced off the plaster. Black spots swam in my vision. I struggled, but he towered over me.

Somewhere in the distance, I could hear my serpent-half thrashing against the net trap Father had set for it. We were weaker apart, and he knew it.

"You will do as I say, go where I say, Pair as I say." He sneered and gestured towards his trap. "No daughter of mine joins with a serpent. Better not to Pair at all."

I would not Pair with some weaker creature, rabbit or lapdog, to suit his perception of what a daughter should be.

A screech ripped from my throat. In the distance, the viper echoed my cry.

We would not be controlled. I bared my fangs and struck.

I shudder at the vivid memory. My throat aches from the phantom scream. I can still taste his blood on my tongue—bitter and smokey, like burning trash. Unable to meld with the trapped serpent, my fangs had carried no venom. They ripped and tore, but in the end, I was no kin killer. Still, it was enough to get away.

Father lives on and we have no choice but to hide.

The serpent quiets, anger turning to longing. We're not meant for this kind of separation. We crave unity, for we are a single soul, split between two bodies. Glancing over my shoulder, I check to see if I'm alone. I'm not supposed to open the window.

I do anyway.

A vast, blunt head nuzzles my hand. I can feel the scars where Father's net burned its scales and for a moment white heat threatens to consume me. This time the anger's mine. The snake mewls, cat-like. I lean further out the window and wrap my arms around its coils. A forked tongue tickles my ears. I struggle to stave off the need to join, to slither as one across the courtyard and explore the shadow-drenched night.

"I can't." My voice catches in my throat. "I almost lost you once."

In the distance, the horizon lightens to soot-smudged gray. It heralds the coming of dawn. Too soon. I tighten my grip on the snake, lay my cheek on its cool hide. Its thoughts pour into me in a rush of images and emotion.

Strength. Love. Hope. Protection.

I release my grip, and it slips away, once again nothing but a river stone driveway beyond the garden gate. With a sigh, I ease the window closed and turn my back on the pending sunrise. My few hours of freedom draw to an end.

The strange smokeless torches—no, light fixtures—blink out as I flip the switch. Every time I wake I find the world has changed a little more. It's odd to experience a timeline in jumps, glimpsing progress in long-legged strides. I must wait my turn, like all the others. It is the way of Sanctuary. We dare not risk more.

The night has brightened enough that I do not need the lights to make my way into the Marble Hall. I weave through the statues that fill the room. The She Wolf curls her lip in a silent snarl, her human cubs at her feet. A dryad dressed in a mantel of blossoms and leaves raises her lithe hand in a frozen wave. The merchant's wife fiddles with a pocket full of bizarre goods. Countless women who sought Sanctuary line the rows, their stone forms so lifelike that if you blink, they seem to breathe. We take turns roaming the halls at night. One at a time, stone softens to flesh. Each who has chosen Sanctuary has her reasons. We never meet, but we are still sisters.

Whispers dance through the hall. Snippets of conversations the statues have stolen from daytime visitors—repurposed to give the stone figures voices. In this way, we share our stories. I hope the throngs bring the right words for me to borrow to tell my sisters of my night's wanderings, the joy I felt to connect with the other half of my soul, if only for a few hours.

I find my empty plinth and duck behind the velvet rope. A hint of pink streams in the window at the end of the hall and my limbs grow heavy. It takes effort to mount the pedestal and strike a regal pose. I always choose something proud—chin raised, fangs bared in defiance. The hints of scales around my eyes harden into snowy marble.

In this stone-chiseled limbo, my soul serpent and I are beyond Father's reach.

Time slows and my vision narrows until only the brass plate at my feet fills my view:

"The Naga of Patala-loka" A Cobra Shifter in carved marble. Circa 850 AD.

A bell jingles in the distant foyer and a line of visitors stream in. The museum has opened for the day.

What You're Left With

FOUR DOWN: a picture or pattern produced by arranging an array of small colored tiles

Six letters. Starts with M.

Everyone thinks the Sunday crossword is the hardest. It's the biggest one, but definitely not the hardest. Sunday through Thursday the puzzles are themed, which makes them easier. It allows me to stay in the same headspace the whole time, instead of having to change gears with every clue.

On Friday, the themes disappear and the hints become more demanding. It's a tough little training ground for what awaits on Saturday. The most arduous, mind bending, complicated word challenge of them all.

I live for Saturdays.

As a point of pride, I do the crossword in pen. I'm no savant, like that guy who does the Saturday puzzle in five and a half minutes whose name I can never remember. My record is eight minutes, nine seconds, no mistakes, no erasing. Not too shabby in the scheme of things.

I like the challenge—reading the clues and the little rush I get when I figure out the answers. But what I really love about the Saturday crossword is that anything goes. History. Art. Pop culture. Classic literature. Sports. Politics. Love.

It's a beautiful, complex *mosaic* that mirrors life.

SEVEN ACROSS: a person or animal having a large amount of excess flesh

Three letters. Ends with T.

Every night I counted out the money I'd earned babysitting over the summer until there was enough.

"Mom? I want to buy a jean jacket." I imagined all the cool patches I'd sew on: a bright yellow smiley face, a peace sign, psychedelic colored flowers, the logos for all my favorite bands.

Mom pursed her lips and looked me up and down.

"Fine."

I started to squeal, but she held up a finger to silence me.

"You have to run a mile without stopping first."

For a moment, I just stared at her, trying to make sense of the words. Not the meaning, but the why. She didn't look at me as she laced up her sneakers.

"I'm going to the track this morning. You'd better come and start training if you want that jacket before school starts."

Resigned, I trudged up to my room to change. I didn't have any workout clothes, so I put on a faded R.E.M. t-shirt and a pair of stiff shorts that I never wore.

Why was Mom making me do this? I'd earned that money and should be able to spend it how I wanted. And jogging? What if someone saw me? Worse, what if someone saw me with my mother? But the jean jacket beckoned. Everyone else had one—I needed one, too.

By the time we reached the track, I was fuming. I'd show her and run that mile on my first try. I took off, rubber slapping the asphalt. Not designed for running, my shorts rode up, but I ignored the discomfort and pushed on.

Mom kept pace beside me, her breathing even.

"Four laps around make a mile."

We made the first turn, side-by-side. Mom's gait lengthened on the straightaway, stepping lightly, the balls of her feel like springs propelling her forward without effort. My feet pounded, flat and heavy, like cement blocks.

On the second turn, I slowed. Face on fire and knees shaking, I gulped air into lungs that didn't want to fill. My ankles ached at the lack of arch support from my flat-soled Keds. Mom was a sadist. There was no other explanation for this torture.

I glared down the endless loop of track and grabbed at the stitch stabbing my side. I wasn't going to finish this lap, let alone three more. Stumbling to a halt, I rested my hands on my knees for a few breaths, then flopped to the ground on my back. Overhead, the cloudless sky filled my vision in a perfect, maddening, cloudless stretch of late summer blue.

Mom's trainers flashed by, and I turned my head to watch her. She spun around, continuing to run backwards. She met my gaze and her eyes said 'you're too old for tantrums.'

"Get up and walk. You need to cool down." She turned back around, never breaking stride. "You can try again tomorrow."

I lugged myself off the asphalt and took a few staggering steps. My t-shirt clung to my back and my thighs burned where they had rubbed together. That's when it hit me.

Mom thought I was *fat.*

SIXTEEN DOWN: the state or feeling of being mortified

Eleven letters. Starts with H, ends with ION.

Propped up on my elbows on my bed, I scribbled answers to the crossword while keeping the cordless phone braced between ear and shoulder.

"I don't know if I want to go, Cathy."

"You have to. It's the Halloween dance!"

Four across. Nothing fit; they all had too many letters.

"Jules? Are you listening to me or are you doing one of your stupid puzzles again?"

I sighed and put the pen down.

"I don't have a costume and I don't dance. What's the point?"

Cathy's huff sounded like a typhoon on the other end of the line.

"It's the first dance of the ninth grade and you're my best friend. Don't make me go alone."

I hated when she played the BFF card. For about thirty seconds, Chatty Cathy was uncharacteristically silent.

I rolled my eyes. "Spill it."

"Well, I think it would be good for you to ditch those giant sweatshirts you always wear. They're not very sexy," she said.

My stomach lurched at the thought.

"What did you have in mind?"

Three nights later, I found myself in the dimly lit school gym, dressed in black jeans and a fitted turtleneck, with a fuzzy tail pinned to my butt. A pair of pointed ears on a headband and whiskers drawn on with eyeliner completed the outfit. Cathy kept grabbing my hands, peeling my crossed arms off my chest.

"You look amazing!"

After the fifth or sixth repetition, I decided to humor her. Our favorite song came on and we joined a gaggle of girls on the dance floor. We laughed and jumped, and for a few moments I forgot I had two left feet and just had fun.

A slow song came on next and in a heartbeat, Cathy, with her long glossy black hair and dimpled smile, had her arms wrapped around the neck of the cutest boy in our year. They swayed in a slow circle. One by one, the other girls paired up with boys and I slunk off to lean against the wall. If only I could disappear into the shadows.

"Hey, Jules."

I jumped. Ross, one of the guys on the JV football team, stood in front of me. He had a chiseled, square jaw and a sandy crewcut. And he knew my name. My mouth went dry.

"Why aren't you dancing?" Ross's raked over me.

I shifted from foot to foot. "No one's asked me."

"Pity."

He inched closer, and suddenly the image of a cat stalking prey filled my mind. Despite the eyeliner whiskers, I felt like the mouse. I glanced around, but no one was paying attention.

Ross's hard blue eyes fixed on my chest, and I squirmed under his gaze.

"I can't believe you've been hiding those tits under your baggy sweatshirts." He leaned against the wall, pinning a lock of my hair under his palm, and leered at me. "Are they real? Can I touch them?"

Panicked, I stomped on his foot, then ducked under his arm to flee. Fire burst across my scalp as a hunk of hair tore free. His laughter chased after me, adding to my *humiliation*. I spent the rest of the evening in the bathroom until Cathy's dad arrived to take us home.

THIRTY-TWO ACROSS: a painful feeling or distress caused by the consciousness of perceived wrong or foolish behavior

Five letters. Starts with SH.

A quiet but insistent knock tapped at the door. I groaned into my pillow and then rolled over to check the clock. 2:37AM. There was only one person who would visit at this hour. I dragged myself out of bed and rummaged in my purse for a mint, then checked the mirror and fluffed my hair. Mascara smudged in dark circles beneath my eyes and I did my best to rub it away.

A muffled voice came through the door.

"Jules? You awake?" Kevin's words slurred. Drunk. I pretended I didn't care.

"Just a minute."

Stripping off the t-shirt and boring beige granny panties I'd worn to bed, I hastily tugged on a silk camisole and a lacy, crimson thong. I turned, scrutinizing my reflection. The lace hugged my curves, a little too tightly to be comfortable. It didn't matter; it would be on the floor before long.

I swaggered across the room with assumed confidence. In the moment, it felt real. An attractive, popular frat boy waited for me on the other side of the door. To kiss and touch and taste. A goofy grin spread across my face, grateful my roommate always went home on the weekends.

Dork.

I wiped away the grin and schooled my features into what I thought was a sultry expression. Think sexy thoughts. I unlatched the chain and opened the door.

Before I had a chance to take a breath, Kevin's mouth closed on mine. His tongue tasted like cigarettes and cheap beer. Teeth snagged my lower lip, and I leaned into the pain. Frantic hands stripped me of silk and lace. We collapsed on my bed in a tangle of limbs.

It was over too soon. Kevin rolled over, uncaring that he'd left me wanting.

"Kev?" He mumbled something, and I took it as a sign to continue. At least he hadn't passed out. My stomach flipped, and the words came out in a rush.

"My cousin's getting married next month and I thought maybe you'd come with me as my date?"

Kevin sniggered. Disappointed, I turned my back on him.

"Are you for real, Jules?" Disgust and contempt warred in his voice.

Of course, he didn't want to be seen with me in public. I was no sorority girl.

He skimmed a hand down my hip, then squeezed, fingers digging into my ample thigh.

"Don't be mad. I just don't think of you that way."

He slid from the bed and tugged on his pants. The door clicked shut behind him, leaving me alone with my *shame.*

SEVENTEEN-DOWN: to lavish insincere praise and compliments upon someone, especially to further one's own interests

Eight letters. Starts with F, ends with RY.

I sipped my black coffee and kept my eyes on the crossword in front of me. There were still twenty minutes or so before I had to be back at work, but I couldn't concentrate on the puzzle. Not with *him* looking at me.

He'd been at my favorite lunch spot every single day this week. I'd take my usual seat at the counter and before my cob salad arrived, he would sidle into the booth in the corner. Tall, broad shouldered, with dark curls that fell into hazel eyes, he was much too handsome to be staring at me. The first time I caught him looking, I checked to see if I had spilled salad dressing on my shirt or had toilet paper stuck to my shoe.

My heart jumped as he grabbed his plate and got up.

He is not coming over here. Oh my God, ohmygod, ohmygod, he is.

He set his untouched burger down on the counter next to my salad and dropped onto the stool.

"Hi, I'm Damon."

The polite reply I was aiming for got stuck somewhere behind my back teeth, and I offered him a weak smile. The pen slipped in my sweaty palm. I cleared my throat and tried again.

"I'm Julie." No one called me that, but in the moment, it sounded more grown up than Jules.

"I see you like the crossword." He laughed, loud and confident, showing off a row of straight white teeth. "I'm shit at them myself. You must be really smart."

"*Flattery* will get you everywhere." The tips of my ears went hot. Gods, he was going to think I was such a fool.

Damon's smile turned coy.

"I certainly hope so." He laid a hand on my arm. "There's a great Thai place that just opened up downtown. Let me take you for dinner sometime."

I could feel my blush spread across my face.

TWENTY-EIGHT ACROSS: feeling or showing envy of someone or their achievements and advantages

Seven letters. Starts with J.

I smoothed white satin over my hips and fussed with my skirt. My chest tightened. I should have gone with the gown with the cap sleeves and the higher neckline, like Mom had suggested. There was too much cleavage, too much skin, too much *me* for this strapless sheath dress. What had I been thinking?

Eels roiled in my stomach. A half hour ago, I'd sent the bridesmaids out into the hall to give myself a moment of peace. Their magpie chattering had brought on the beginning of a headache. Alone in the dressing room at the back of the church, I paced, awkward in the heels

I was unused to wearing. Another foolish choice. The mental image of me tripping over my own feet as I walked down the aisle filled my head.

"Get a grip, Jules. This is your day. Every bride is a beautiful, graceful angel." I snorted. What a load of crap. Still, for whatever reason, it calmed my nerves a little.

I cracked the door to tell the girls I was ready for them to come back in. Their whispered voices echoed too loudly in the marble vestibule. Cathy held court, the other three girls ringed around her like courtesans. My once BFF and I hadn't talked much since high school, but I had felt obligated to ask her to be in the wedding. As always, she looked like a model: perfect hair, perfect skin, an air of easy confidence. Heads turned whenever she walked into a room, now more than ever.

Cathy leaned towards the girls and pitched her voice low.

"I just don't know what Damon sees in her, you know?" The bridesmaids tittered.

"Cathy! You're so bad!"

"You're right though. Who would have imagined a chubby, ugly thing like her landing a guy like that?"

"What a waste of a hottie."

Cathy gave them a wicked grin, encouraging another round of backbiting.

I backed away from the door, eyes smarting. Grabbing a tissue, I blotted them before my eyeliner could run. Fingers trembling, I tried to convince myself they were just *jealous*. A snarky little voice in the back of my head told me their jibes were all true.

FORTY-ONE DOWN: a sudden, intuitive perception of, or insight into, the reality or essential meaning of something

Eight letters. Starts with E, ends with ANY

I turned off the engine and coasted into the driveway. If Damon didn't hear me pull in, I could sit in the car for a few minutes; psych myself up before going inside. He'd been sleeping off a hangover when I had left for work this morning, and I prayed he wouldn't be in a foul mood. Sweat trickled down my back as the car warmed. It would soon become unbearable. I braced myself and went in.

The house was dark, shades drawn, the only light the flickering blue of the TV coming from the living room. Not a good sign. I hung up my purse and nudged the dimmer switch so the kitchen lights came on half way.

"Hun?" I stepped softly, trying not to make too much noise. "I'm home. I can start dinner if you're hungry."

Damon, dressed in a stained tank top and sweats, grunted and flipped the channels. He didn't bother to look at me, just took another pull on his beer. I retreated to the kitchen.

I checked the fridge, but it was mostly filled with cheap IPAs and expired condiments. Damon had promised he'd do the grocery shopping today. I should have known better and stopped on my way from work, but he didn't like it when I got home late. He'd grill me—just how long does it fucking take to buy milk and bread, Jules? He never believed my answers.

Rummaging in the cupboard, I found a jar of sauce and put water on for pasta. I sighed. No matter how meager the serving on my plate, I expected a repeat lecture on the carbs going straight to my hips.

"What the fucking hell is that?"

Damon's roar startled me, and I dropped the wooden spoon I was holding. It fell to the floor with a clatter. My eyes darted around the kitchen as I tried to find what was out of place, where I'd made some kind of mistake. Everything seemed normal.

"You wore that to work today?"

What was wrong with what I was wearing? I glanced down at the demure cotton sundress. Too short? No, it fell halfway down my calves.

Too much cleavage? No, the modest scoop neckline covered everything up to my collarbones.

"I don't understand. W-what's wrong with my dress?" I tried to make my voice soothing and gentle.

"What are you, some sort of whore? Wearing a sleeveless dress to work, trying to impress the salesmen? Stupid slut."

I wanted to say—you used to trust me—but I knew better than to provoke him.

"Take. It. Off." He growled the words.

It was better not to argue, or the shouting could last for hours. Mute, I shimmied out of the dress and handed it over.

Damon grabbed a knife from the butcher block. Again and again, the knife tore into the fabric until there was nothing left but a heap of tattered rags. I stood there, shivering in my underclothes, not daring to speak. Damon stared at me, the knife in his hand, breathing hard and eyes wild. For a dozen heartbeats, we stayed that way.

The pasta boiled over.

"Clean that mess up." He tossed the knife in the sink, grabbed a beer from the fridge, and went back into the living room.

It wasn't until hours later, locked away in the guest bedroom, that I had my *epiphany*. It was just one more way to control me.

"At least he doesn't hit me," I whispered to myself.

FIFTY ACROSS: the process of training or accustoming a person to behave in a certain way or believe proposed ideas, regardless of their truth

Twelve letters. Starts with COND.

My childhood bedroom looked exactly the same as I remembered. Pink bedspread, posters of bands sporting acid-washed jeans and teased hair, bookshelves filled with dogeared romances and mystery novels. It even smelled the same, like the smoky vanilla perfume I used to wear in junior high. It was a trick of the mind, though. They didn't make it anymore.

I tossed my bag on the bed. How sad my entire life fit into one shabby suitcase. There wasn't much to take—some clothes, a few personal items. I left behind all the photos and jewelry and "I'm sorry" gifts. I didn't want the memories of the screaming, the jealousy, the humiliation, and the shame.

One of my old crossword books lay on the desk; an old friend waiting for my return. I sat down and flipped to a new puzzle. My pen flew across the page as I solved the clues. It scratched against the paper at a feverish pace.

"Knock, knock." Mom leaned in the doorway, but I kept working. She watched me for a minute.

"Dinner's almost ready, if you want to come down. Baked salmon and green beans." She made a little clucking noise with her tongue. "Dad wanted steak and mashed potatoes with gravy, but I told him now you were home, it would do us all some good to eat healthy."

I didn't reply. The pen filled letters in the boxes almost of its own volition. Last clue.

"I never understood your obsession with crossword puzzles," Mom said.

I glanced at the timer on my phone. Eight minutes, seven seconds. A new record.

Carefully, I put the pen down and closed the book. I took a deep breath and looked up. Her hair was grayer, but she still ran three miles a day. She was eternal.

"I like doing the puzzles, Mom. It's the only time that I really feel like me."

Fat. Ugly. Stupid. Worthless.

"If you strip that away, all I have left is *conditioning*."

Longing for the Sea

At sunset, they went to the shore.

The mother, a large bundle over her shoulder, held her son's hand, reminding him to keep his voice down. No one came here anymore, to this tiny cove accessible only when the tide was low on the night of a full moon. Any other time, the waves swallowed the beach and battered against the rocks. The splintered hull of an old boat lay partially buried in the sand as a reminder of the danger. Still, on this night, she guided the boy along the narrow track that switched-backed down the cliff. Though the light was failing, her feet knew the way.

When they reached the crescent beach, the boy wanted to splash bare toes in the surf, to let the waves suck the sand out from beneath his feet. He reveled in small discoveries, at home in the briny water. Tugging at his mother's arm, he bent to point out bits of shells and polished stones and scuttling crabs trapped in the tide pools.

"Hush now, child. They're coming." Her voice was a murmured breeze over the sounds of the sea.

She knew just the right moment—when the sky streaked melon and crimson and the sun flirted with the horizon. The pair stayed silent, and before long, sleek bodies surfaced. Liquid brown eyes scanned the beach. Wary. Curious.

The boy's heart thrummed, and he held his breath.

Cautiously, the creatures came ashore, flippers leaving deep furrows in the sand. The molten sun went to its rest, and the moon began to climb into the sky. One by one, the seals shivered and dropped their pelts. Powerful tails split into pairs of graceful legs. Whiskers disappeared. Pale arms stretched over wild heads of dripping, tangled hair.

In awe, the boy stared. Women stood where the seals had been. They combed each other's hair in the silver moonlight and crooned wordless tunes. Their songs haunted the night, a fluid sound that twisted with the tide and pulsed with the waves. The boy thought it seemed both familiar and strangely uncanny, like some half-remembered dream.

The selkies gathered around the boy's mother. They touched her simple homespun dress and frowned. Insistent hands opened her bundle and a soft, mottled brown skin shook loose. Voices chattered. Words the boy instinctively knew meant *sister* and *home*, but sounded like neither.

One of the women studied the child. He trembled as she explored his face with her fingers, cool and silky, yet strong as the tide. She stroked his hair and gave him a sad smile. The selkies whispered to each other.

Half human. No pelt.

The boy looked up at his mother, deep into her eyes, and saw how she longed for the sea. The mother looked back, uncertain how to make an impossible choice. She clutched her hide to her chest as salt spray mingled with the tears on her cheeks, unable to speak.

A matronly selkie with ropes of white hair flowing over her shoulders stepped forward. She bared sharp teeth, and the boy shrank back. Quick as lightning, she bit down and tore a strip from her own pelt. She handed it to the boy's mother. Each of the selkies followed the stern matriarch's lead, ripping a ragged piece from their own seal hides and making their offerings. Someone conjured up a sea urchin spine, needle sharp.

The boy's mother squared her shoulders as she yanked long strands of hair from her own head, then took the spine, and began to sew. Piece by piece, the patchwork pelt grew. The makeshift needle pricked her fingers, but she ignored the pain. She raced against the moon and the rising tide. All around her, the selkies resumed their night song, weaving their magic into the skin.

Hurry. Hurry. The sun rises!

A blush kissed the far edge of the sea. Blood dotted the mother's hands, a sacrifice given freely to the work. The moon sunk into the sea, a scant fingernail of silver left visible. It was finished. The selkies wrapped their skins around themselves. In a blink, tails and flippers returned to the sea.

The mother dropped the newly sewn hide over her son's shoulders and hoped. His eyes widened as it molded to his flesh. Fingers and toes fused. She jerked her own skin around her, desperate to make the change before the sun cleared the horizon.

Out in the bay, seals barked in encouragement. The mother seal and her cub barked back and dove into the sea. Lithe bodies rolled in the surf, tails slapping playfully as the selkies welcomed their lost sister and her child into the fold.

By the time full dawn arrived, the tide had risen to swallow the small beach, erasing the footprints in the sand. No one came to this cove anymore. There was no need.

I Won't be Swimming Today

There are jellyfish in the fucking pool. Yes, I'm blind, but I know they're there, though not the same way I know you're looking at me askance about that f'bomb. That's just intuition. I really don't want to hear any tired rhetoric that insists women of a certain age should be demure and wear cardigans in July. If you haven't noticed, I'm rocking pink hair and tattoos. I'm fifty, not dead.

Anyway, back to the jellyfish. Wait. I should probably start at the beginning and tell you about losing my sight. I mean, I can't really talk about *Sight* until we get through the whole blindness thing.

Early last year, everything went to hell. At first, I thought it was just a perimenopause symptom, loath as I was to admit it. Trying to figure out hormones can make a person bat shit crazy. And guess what? Blurry vision is one of the million symptoms they don't tell you about. I'm pretty sure it's a way to devalue women as we age, keeping us off kilter and uncertain about what our bodies are going to throw at us next. But that's a whole other story.

So, yes, my vision slowly started to deteriorate. It got to a point where my arms weren't long enough to hold my phone at a comfortable distance for watching those adorable puppy reels on Instagram. And honestly, I needed those videos to deal with the dumpster fire that is the world. You know what I'm talking about; I don't need to spell it out. Besides, this isn't that kind of story.

Enter the "readers." Just the drugstore kind, 1x magnification. They helped for a while, and I sprinkled them everywhere, like tortoise-rimmed confetti. A pair at my desk, a pair on the coffee table. Glasses on the bed stand for doom scrolling, and in the kitchen for recipe reading, and in the car for taking into the grocery store. (Why do they make the ingredient lists on packages so small?) Eventually, I graduated to the 1.5x magnification, then 2x.

After that, things took a disturbing turn. Colors started fading. The crimson poppies in my garden turned dusky rose, and my favorite emerald earrings lost their luster. Before long, everything looked like a sepia photograph. Losing color made my stomach hurt. I'm more of a Kandinsky girl than Monet, and I lived for viridian and cerulean and magenta and carmine.

Then sepia turned monochrome gray.

I went to specialist after specialist, but no one could find anything wrong with me. I panicked. Western medicine had failed, so I tried herbalists and Reiki and acupuncture. When that didn't work, I tried priests and monks and spiritualists. I prayed to gods I'd never believed in, promising to change my hedonistic, heathen ways if only they saved me from a world of consummate darkness.

Either the gods didn't exist, or they decided I wasn't devout enough. Either could be true. I've never been very good at faith. I like facts and science; things I can see. I was well and truly fucked.

On my fiftieth birthday, the lights went out.

Being blind sucked, and the hits kept coming. Apparently, Director of Marketing and Design wasn't a thing they let you keep doing once you lose your sight. Like a racehorse who stumbled out of the starting gate at the Belmont Stakes, I was put out to pasture. Now that I think about it, the ADA might have had something to say about that, but at the time I was too despondent to think about my rights as a disabled person.

Disabled. Person with a disability. Differently abled. No matter what you call it, it still blows.

I've always been an overachiever, and the "early retirement" hit hard. For weeks, I woke up at six on the dot out of habit, only to have the realization I had nowhere to go crash down on me. For weeks after that, I stayed in bed. What was the point of getting up, only to meander through the house, stubbing my toes on the corners of the table after finding myself in the dining room when I was aiming for the kitchen?

Feeling sorry for myself became a full-time hobby. Well, that and bourbon. I'll admit, for a time, the Old Fashioned became my drink of choice. Screw water. I had a rocks glass going at all times—cocktail hour, in the evening, before bed, for breakfast. I was aiming for an all-day fettle of comfortably numb but managed to give myself the beginnings of an ulcer. That was fun. (In case you're bad at subtext, that's sarcasm.) Instead of buying stock in Tums, I gave the hooch up.

What? No, I didn't have anyone to "take care of me." I come from a long line of women who fucking take care of themselves. Well, except my mom. She took a swan dive off a cliff when she turned fifty. I'm pretty sure it's not a coincidence. I was off building a career, kicking ass and taking names at the time. When you're twenty-five, narcissism is pretty much baked in. Doing my thing seemed more important than whatever Mom was up to. Regret is an evil bitch. Though, not sure she would have talked to me about all the weirdness anyway.

But I would have liked to have had the chance to try.

I've never really been into the whole relationship thing, either. Nowadays, there's a label for everything. It's all gotta fit in the appropriate box. You'd probably paint me as "aromantic." Don't get me wrong, I enjoy a little hokey-pokey now and then. Again, fifty, not dead. I just want my partners to go home afterward. After a while, though, I found the kind of people who are just looking for a quick booty call didn't really care if I got off, too. Why expend all that energy if I literally have to take matters into my own hands?

And before you ask, no, I've never had any desire for kids. I'm not sure why society thinks that's a moral failing. It's not like the population's going to take a hit if I don't procreate. Besides, I like the life I built, and that should be good enough. Stop being so nosey.

I feel like we've gone off topic. Not sure my sex life and lack of maternal urges are relevant. Enough to say, I was on my own before the world went dark, and so I had to try to navigate it on my own afterward.

Once I got over my blindness pity party, I started figuring shit out. Probably out of spite. I remember the day a neighbor said I shouldn't go out walking on my own. So, I got myself a tippity-tappity cane, and took over the sidewalks like a boss. Tech has come a long way for the "visually impaired," too. (That's the polite way of saying stone-blind.) I have software that reads books and websites to me. Braille is so 1985. I have speech-to-text and grocery delivery and a million other assistive technologies. It's not the same as seeing, but it makes the world navigable.

Still, being blind is shitty. Zero stars; do not recommend.

Then I got the *Sight.*

Remember, I said I was all about the science? A year ago, I would have doubled-down on that. I'd never been into all that paranormal hooey. Tell me you saw a ghost? I'd call it a hallucination. Believe in fairies and unicorns? I'd say you had an overabundance of imagination. Fearful of the boogeyman? I'd say, pull up your big girl panties. The only monsters out there are the psychopaths wearing human faces. Have you seen the crap people do to each other? Even now, I maintain people are the *worst.* But don't get me started on that. You probably don't have the time for a tangential rant about racism and misogyny and bigotry and ageism...and all the fucked up stuff that comes from the righteously small minded.

Back to the map. The *Sight* didn't start small and ramp up, like a reverse of the decline. It came all at once with a wooly mammoth in the garden. He was more Snuffleupagus than a majestic Pleistocene era beast, and he was surprised as hell that I could see him. I thought I was having a stroke myself.

He looked at me with impossibly wide eyes, and I stared right back. Then, after what felt like a fortnight of centuries, he said, "Hey. I'm Bob. Sorry to intrude. Just wanted to smell the flowers for a bit."

I couldn't see them, mind you, but I could tell the poppies were in bloom. They have a distinct spicy, earthy scent and the air was full of their particular bouquet. Now, I know you're going to ask if I was high, but I wasn't. They weren't those kind of poppies. Growing the opiate type is illegal. Well, for a time, there was a group of Shakers in New Hampshire who had a special allowance to grow the *medicinal* kind, but the last one of those badass ladies died in the early nineties. (I know, I'm just full of useless knowledge.)

All that to say, my mind was clear, the flowers smelled nice, there was a gods damned talking wooly mammoth in the garden, and I could absolutely see him. He sniffed and smelled and appreciated the landscaper's green thumb for a bit, then wandered off, leaving me, once again, in total darkness.

After that, things got hella weird.

I wish I could say that the Sight manifested in a helpful way. Maybe kaleidoscopic auras shimmering around living things, so I could have conversations with people without staring off into no-man's-land like a weirdo.

No fucking chance.

The next thing to blow my mind was the flying whale. Blue whales aren't really blue, they're really more grayish with white bellies. And there she was, floating across the black expanse of sky at noon. I could say I knew it was midday by the strength of the sun's rays on my face. But that would be hogwash. I knew because my watch beeped. That whole *once you go blind, your other senses get more acute* business is unadulterated fiction. Sure, you rely on them more, but you don't suddenly have the capacity to hear at frequencies only dogs do. Believe that, and I have a delightful waterfront property in the Everglades to sell you.

Anyway, the whale was something else. She swam through the sky, diving and rolling, like a two-hundred-ton ballerina. You'd think something of that size would be awkward and clumsy, but she wasn't. I wish I had a fraction of her grace. I was a klutz, covered in bruises I had no idea how I got, from way before I lost my sight. It's just worse now. (Probably good I can't see myself in the mirror, covered in purple, green, and fading yellow polka-dots.)

I watched the whale for hours, pretty much mesmerized as she sky danced for me in a private showing. Here's a bit of advice for you—it's ok to cry when you see something so mind blowing, indescribably breathtaking. Don't let anyone tell you otherwise or you'll grow up emotionally stunted.

Eventually, the whale moved on, and my tears dried. Still, I sat on the garden bench, my ass going numb on the hard planks, on the chance (and hope) she came back. Let's face it—after six months alone in the dark, seeing an air-whale ballet was probably the best thing that could have happened to me.

The whole thing kinda broke my brain, though, and it took a couple days for the natural questions of *how* and *why* to occur to me. Once I decided I wasn't having a nervous breakdown brought on my inexplicable blindness and hormones.

I asked the Google, on incognito mode, of course. Not surprising, that was a bust. There are a boatload of crackpots on the interwebs and I spent more days than I should probably admit hunting them all down. And dismissing their stories as self-aggrandizing malarkey and hoaxes that even the most gullible wouldn't believe. Perhaps they were just imaginative, lonely folx, looking to have an interesting story so that people might pay attention to them. It was pretty sad, to be honest.

With no answers from my research, there was only one thing left I could do. I was going to have to call my Gran.

Gran's what you would call a bit of a character. That's the nice way of saying she's a total nutter. Mom never talked about my father. When she did, she called him "the sperm donor." (That would be a drunken mistake, not a clinic and a turkey baster.) I never knew his side of the family. Gran is Mom's mom. We never spent a lot of time with her either. She and Mom didn't really get along because Gran's a witch. For most of my life, I thought that was a euphemism, but suddenly I wondered if Mom had been speaking literally.

The conversation went a little like this:

Me: Hi Gran, it's me, Delta. (Yes, that's my name. What of it?)

Gran: You're calling about the Sight. 'Bout time.

That's right, "about time" like she was expecting me all along. Come to find out, she had been.

Long story shorter, the women in my family have Gifts. Not reasonable gifts, like perky boobs that defy gravity even after fifty or the ability to do complex math equations in our heads. Nope. We got the *Sight*. Apparently, it's different for everyone. Gran has the ability to *See* short distances into the future. Not lottery numbers or anything life changing, more like knowing when the phone is about to ring or when a visitor might stop by in enough time to tidy up real quick and start a pot of tea.

Mom had a tough one. She could *See* the manifestation of people's true selves. Not their aura or anything. Gran had scoffed at that idea and called it rubbish. No, Mom could *See* the fire that burned in the greedy CEO's gut, and the fractures in a stranger's heart. She could *See* the phantom handprint on a woman's cheek, even when the victim refused to admit her husband was a violent asshole. It broke Mom's heart.

I don't blame her, but I wished she'd talked to me about it. I wish she hadn't felt so alone...

Sorry, what was I saying before I got all maudlin on you? Right, the *Sight*. So Gran had a useful little skill, Mom a demon. I got all the weird creatures, from teal bunnies the size of lions to fire-maned night mares that galloped through the stars. (Not nightmares, that's a different thing altogether.) There are the things that are just too outlandish for the human eye to take in. Or maybe for the brain to comprehend. It takes the *Sight* to make it all out. You wouldn't believe the things I've seen.

Unless you've got the Gift and you've been humoring me all this time. No? Then, I'll continue.

So, that's the *what*. As for the *how*, Gran says it's hereditary. A rare gene that expresses like red hair and freckles. Seems legit. I mean, why not? It's a good enough explanation for me. She might have just made that up, though, knowing I wouldn't have accepted "it's magic" for an answer. She couldn't really tell me why I had to fucking go blind in order to *See*. But at my age, I've come to accept that some things are simply inexplicable. It saves a lot of time and angst and Tylenol.

Anyway, I suppose that takes me back to the beginning of all this. I'm not swimming today, even though it's hotter than Satan's armpit out there, because there are polychromatic jellyfish in the pool. They kind of look like gelatinous rainbows the size of dinner plates. I'm not entirely sure how long they're gonna stick around. They're more interested in floating in the deep end than chatting. And I for one, am not so rude as to interrupt their soak. Some things, like fifty-year-old, pink-haired, tattooed, single, childless, potty-mouthed women and multi-hued jellyfish in the pool, are best left alone.

The Wise Internal Voice

Be watchful of voices that shout shouldn't, mustn't, don't.

They said she shouldn't climb up the fire escape and whisper conversations with the night sky. It was one thing to perch on the roof's edge, feet dangling, and look down on the city below, taking in the glow of neon lights. But who was she to speak so intimately to the stars?

They told her she mustn't touch the sidewalk trees growing in their iron cages. Couldn't she see how she made their roots quest upwards and fracture the concrete? Leave the trees—and the sidewalks—to the professionals, with their chemicals and their saws.

They insisted she oughtn't sing and dance with pixies. Not even when a summer squall left rainbowed puddles on the oil-slicked asphalt, just perfect for rhythmic splashing. No matter how much it filled the hollowness inside. Didn't she know the fae were pesky critters with their toothpick swords and feral grins? She might as well cavort with rats.

Also, don't cavort with rats. Even if their stories of subway adventures were bold and thrilling. Nothing good could come of it. People would talk.

Be wary of couldn't and be suspicious of won't.

They swore They couldn't tell her where the wild night-mares ran, with their otherworldly eyes and twilight manes. She only wanted to watch the fae horses deliver their dreams, hooves thundering across the velvet gloaming.

They wouldn't share where the wind spirits came from, nor where they blew off to when the storm clouds disappeared. They cried crocodile tears and told her it was for her own good, to keep her safe in the Here and Now. Elsewhere and Tomorrow were dangerous places where proper young ladies would never yearn to go.

In reality, They dismissed her as just a girl. A nobody girl with crooked teeth and frizzy hair who wanted more than was her right.

Don't overstep. Go watch makeup tutorials, or shop with a friend. That's what normal girls do. Didn't she want to fit in?

Look for labels and learn how to decipher their disdain.

They called her feisty when They meant difficult. Honey-coated tongues said persistent and inquisitive, with an aftertaste of stubborn and meddlesome. They would make her doubt her value, delivering veiled insults with used car salesmen smiles.

Be demure; be reserved; be conventional.

They told her who to be without seeing her as she was.

Walk away instead of breaking.

They wailed and wrung Their hands when she gathered up the pixies and the rats and took the last bus to where the asphalt ended and the switchgrass began. How dare she turn her back on Their shelter built of couldn'ts and won'ts? They'd only wanted the best for her. To make her like Them.

She dropped her phone, abandoning it in the hazy liminal space between Here and There. They filled the tiny screen with don'ts and can'ts she would never read.

Trailing her fingers over leaf and stem, she waded through the tall grass toward a future of maybes, what-ifs, and possibilities. Where only green had been before, a sea of white and silver sprang up in her wake. The air filled with the heady perfume of night-blooming jasmine and hope.

Look forward, never back.

Overhead, the stars sang their approval.

Acknowledgements

Writing is a solitary endeavor. And yet it isn't. I'm grateful to have an amazing tribe. Naming every person who has supported this journey would take forever, however, I'd be remiss for not highlighting a few. I promise, I'll make this mercifully short.

Many thanks to Myna Chang, Lisa Fox, and Aeryn Rudel. It is a gift to have a team of beta readers who get me, even when I'm not being very clear, and who aren't afraid to lay on the tough love when necessary.

To Charlie Rogers, thank you for being the kind of scribble sibling who checks in on me, who sees me when I'm not at my best, and is somehow able to find the right words to encourage me when I'm about ready to give up.

LF and WAB crews, you are a never-ending source of community, cheerleading, commiseration, and knowledge. Thanks to Di Brown for inviting me to the former, and to the latter, I appreciate you all for not kicking me out when I crashed the party uninvited.

Much love to my parents, who raised me to believe I could be whoever I wanted, even if they haven't always agreed with the choices I've made. There is something freeing about being given the chance to make your own mistakes. I always knew, though, there was a safety net available to me, even if I was too stubborn to use it.

Finally, I am humbled and grateful to all of you, dear readers. I'm not here for accolades or to become rich and famous. I just want to tell stories. However, time and again, the love from readers simply blows me away. Thank you for coming along on this journey with me. There are still more tales to tell and I hope we'll keep doing this together for some time to come.

Publication History

- "SafeChip(TM)" The Corona Book of Science Fiction
- "A Taste of Online Dating" MetaStellar
- "For Want of a Conversation" Writers Workout 72 Hours of Insanity, Volume 10
- "To Join a Brotherhood" Uncharted
- "Never-ending Dawn" Flash Point Science Fiction
- "Knock, Knock" Intrepidus Ink
- "Sanctuary" Writers Workout 72 Hours of Insanity, Volume 11
- "What You're Left With" Writers Workout 72 Hours of Insanity, Volume 8
- "Longing for the Sea: *originally published as* "To Long for the Sea" Iron Faerie Publishing Merfolk Anthology
- "The Wise Internal Voice" Intrepidus Ink

Also by MM Schreier

Monstrosity, Humanity
Bruised, Resilient

Watch for more at https://www.mmschreier.com.

About the Author

MM Schreier is a classically trained vocalist who took up writing as therapy for a mid-life crisis.

Whether contemporary or speculative fiction, favorite stories are dark and rich in sensory details. Weird twists abound—fiction with just enough truth thrown in to make folks question. Or perhaps that's non-fiction that's somehow gotten twisted up in imagination.

A firm believer that people are not always exclusively right- or left-brained, in addition to creative pursuits, Schreier is on the Leadership Team for a robotics company and tutors maths and science to at-risk youth. After years of living in the Great White North, Schreier and a very spoiled Labrador Retriever have inched a bit south to become beach bums at Chilly by the Sea.

Read more at https://www.mmschreier.com.